A PECULIAR FEELING OF
restlessness

A PECULIAR FEELING OF
Restlessness

four chapbooks of short short fiction by four women

Amy L. Clark | Elizabeth Ellen | Kathy Fish | Claudia Smith

Rose Metal Press

2008

Rose Metal Press, Inc.
P.O. Box 1956
Brookline, MA 02446
rosemetalpress@gmail.com
www.rosemetalpress.com

Library of Congress Control Number: 2008923766

ISBN: 978-0-9789848-3-0

Cover and interior design by Melissa Gruntkosky
Cover typefaces: Filosofia and Gill Sans
Interior typeface: Sabon
See "A Note About the Type" for more information about the type.

This book is manufactured in the United States of America and printed on acid-free paper.

Table of Contents

Preface

Wanting by Amy L. Clark, *Sixteen Miles Outside of Phoenix* by Elizabeth Ellen, *Laughter, Applause. Laughter, Music, Applause* by Kathy Fish, *The Sky Is a Well* by Claudia Smith— four excellent titles for four excellent collections of short short fiction. When Rose Metal Press decided to publish all four chapbooks together, we knew we needed an equally excellent title for the entire project. But for the longest time, we couldn't come up with one that seemed up to the task. In the interim, we referred to the anthology as 4x4, a phrase with a rugged and powerful sound we liked, but which ultimately seemed a bit generic for a set of chapbooks that was anything but. We toyed with the idea of the number four for ages—Quart, Quarto, Quartier, Quartern, Quarter points, Compass rose, Directionals, Quad, Quadratic, A fourth, Four points, Four corners, Four square, Four circle, Four leaves (quatrefoil), Four-part harmony, Quartet, Quarter horse, Quarter house, Quarter moon, Lunar, Waxing quarter, Quatrain, Quarter whole, A dollar, Full moon, 4/4 time, 4 measure—but this turned out to be fruitless.

We experimented with pulling phrases from the individual collections—Each Thing I Could Do in Under Three Minutes; Options for Young Women; Behind Their Odd Shadow; It Seemed Like the Thing to Do; We'll Remember Him When the Revolution Comes; I Do Not Mean Metaphorically; A Controlled Fall into Acute Longing; Intense Study of Trial & Error; Forever Naughty, Forever in Peril; Baby Boy, I'd Just as Soon Punch You in the Gut—but again, none of these seemed quite right.

We decided to shelve the task of titling for a while as we moved ahead with design options and layouts, and as the time to go to press drew closer, we began to despair of ever settling on the precisely right name. We sent a pleading email to our four authors asking for their suggestions. "And as for titles, I have only seen my own work, but there must be a line in someone's story that has something to do with hybrids, or multiplicity, or the power of words," wrote Amy L. Clark. So we went back again, and this time we found it, there in the middle of Elizabeth Ellen's collection: *A Peculiar Feeling of Restlessness*.

The phrase struck us as right because it seems to describe how we felt when we read each of these manuscripts for the first time and how we still feel when we read them again: like we are obviously in the presence of talented and engaging intellects, writers so skilled at immersing you in their words that you finish reading feeling almost as though you've run a race or been dancing or practiced yoga or some other activity that is physically and mentally good and challenging. These succinct stories pratically shake with underlying tension and energy. The fact that we had this feeling after we read each one of these collections during our first annual short short fiction chapbook contest in 2006 made us realize that all of these chapbooks needed to be published and published together. We were delighted with contest judge Ron Carlson's selection of Claudia Smith's *The Sky Is a Well* as the winner of the contest, but the beauty of being a small, independent press is that when your contest spills over with talented entries, you can say, as we did, let's not let these other chapbooks we love slip away. Thus, we hatched the plan that has resulted in the book you're currently holding: *A Peculiar Feeling of Restlessness: Four Chapbooks of Short Short Fiction by Four Women.*

As we read through the large number of high quality contest submissions, we noticed that, even though there are many exciting short shorts being written by both men and women, much of the work that thrilled us happened to be written by female authors. Few would dispute that Virginia Woolf was right when she wrote, "A woman must have money and a room of her own if she is to write fiction." Women who write short shorts seem to have discovered that a woman can, if she needs to, get by with less money and a pretty small room as she writes short short fiction. The challenges of the form appear to be well-suited to their lives as wives, mothers, teachers, and professionals, and Clark, Ellen, Fish, and Smith are masters at distilling complicated relationships into a page or two of text, at making a single scene resonate with larger meaning. As a female-run press, Rose Metal is honored and pleased to have these four women together under the cover of one book.

Abigail Beckel & Kathleen Rooney
February 2008

Introduction:
The Parts My Grandmother Didn't Tell

By Pia Z. Ehrhardt

I GREW UP AROUND WOMEN who held the room: my violinist mother with her cool beauty, elegant and distracted by something outside of us; my never-married godmother, with her array of quarterback/Bohemian/mobster/biker boyfriends who came and went; and my father's mother, who told twisty, charming stories about growing up in a medieval town in Central Italy, the youngest of six, with brothers who gambled and ran around with fallen women and sisters who baked bread and fell in love with boys who died in the war. These stories, I believe, were given to us with love and they held me rapt. I was an eager heart in the audience of my Nonna, but as I grew up and made mistakes, fell, got hurt, hurt back, felt shame, began lying, I realized that, maybe, these stories were varnished to protect her family and her privacy and to distract us with the music of the telling.

The first stories I wrote as an undergrad transcribed what I'd heard around my grandmother's dinner table. I chose to write what I knew would please my grandmother, because, at nineteen I didn't think I had anything personal to say yet. I designated myself the family archivist, the recorder-on-paper of what I feared would be lost when my Nonna died. But something happened as I tried to write down what I'd heard her recount so many times: the stories and the characters began to stray. I filled in the spaces that baffled me with made-up stuff, and I usurped the point-of-view. I drew my own conclusions about the fallen women—fallen? from where?—the cuckolded men, the spinsters behind drawn curtains, all of whom seemed stuck inside my grandmother's renditions, like spiders in resin.

And where was my grandmother in these stories? When would the teller become the told-upon? Were her entertaining rehashes a sleight-of-hand to distract from the immediate concerns of her own heart? Did she understand "fallen women"? Had she only loved my grandfather? After her older brother molested a family member, why did she only tell the story of the fifteen patents he held with an eighth grade education? She died holding onto her secrets, and I began writing in search of other people's, including my own.

The four brilliant chapbooks that make up *A Peculiar Feeling of Restlessness* are disarmingly, unabashedly intimate collections by women who know how to tell a story and aren't afraid to drag the unspoken out into the light of day. What an uneasy pleasure it is to read—in depth—the work of Amy L. Clark, Elizabeth Ellen, Kathy Fish, and Claudia Smith. These women are not practicing the oral tradition; theirs are not stories to listen to over dessert and coffee with grappa. They are written for the page; late night shots of Jägermeister, belly to the bar, sent over by a stranger.

The stories in Amy L. Clark's collection *Wanting* are satisfying, wise, and often funny. Time rocks forward so her narrators can look back over a shoulder at the next boyfriend, at a dentist-lover, at Jason Jacob, a future date-rapist whose mother dies taking him to the hospital: "The car rolled four times. Presumably, Jason watched her die while they were trapped inside the car. Everyone had known for as long as we could remember that: he was alive and she was not when the ambulance got there." Are people what they choose to be, or what their choices make them?

Then there are the tumbling, courageous meditations of Elizabeth Ellen, who, in *Sixteen Miles Outside of Phoenix,* writes unremittingly about the phantom pain of separated hearts, about daughters who tell their mothers "You're not a very good girlfriend," and "I'm afraid of never seeing you again" or a poet-lover who bears "little resemblance to the photo on the jacket of the book," about wanting, getting, losing, retreating, but remembering: "For three seconds you actually believed he was moving back, that once more he would be on the same side of the Mississippi as you, and that surely you were the reason for this sudden relocation."

In *Laughter, Applause. Laughter, Music, Applause*, Kathy Fish creates vivid, crowded dioramas of kids left unattended while mothers wave down the sky, of an *auteur* sister chasing her hapless jock brother with a video camera, or of reunited siblings eating omelets before they go to the sudden funeral of their nephew. Her short pieces contain a novel's worth of tensions; the lines are deft, precise, necessary: "'We'd better hustle. We're supposed to be there by 10:30,' he's saying this to Rob. They're to be the pallbearers. We all go quiet, like we've been switched off."

And then there's Claudia Smith's prize-winning chapbook *The Sky Is a Well,* where childhood is filled with quotidian things—Dairy Queen Blizzards and dingleberries, Avon lotion and brown ribbon shoelaces—that turn into emblems of risk and disappointment. Children wait outside while their parents fuck, beaten mothers take refuge in their daughters, fathers loom. A young girl warns: "There's going to be a solar eclipse this Saturday. You're supposed to look at it through cardboard, with your back turned. I tell her that's what I'm going to do. But I intend to look at it directly."

I like to look into these stories and try to guess on which sentence the writer began. What ignited this short short's flame? A memory, a regret, an answer to a question that's never added up, an exit, an entrance, a peripheral bit of kindness? And how many times did the writer get up from her desk for Cheez-Its rather than look at the eclipse directly, only to sit her butt back down again and finish what she'd started? I'm thinking a box full.

These works are short but not soon over. They insist on their size, demanding to be read forwards and then backwards, as lines register and you double take on things people don't usually say but mean. It will take you a few minutes to read one and then an age to forget.

What rattles around inside the people we think we know? What deeper truths? Is there such a thing as a secret that needs keeping? Not in my book. When my grandmother was dying and in hospice, the last person she called out for was her mother. She raised her arms to be lifted up like a child, and I thought, she's always been someone's child, a good child who kept the family's business the family's business. I like to think that my Nonna had more understanding than she knew what to do with, and that the unflinching stories you will read in *A Peculiar Feeling of Restlessness* have the heart and the urgency to worry about the parts my grandmother left out.

LAUGHTER, APPLAUSE. LAUGHTER, MUSIC, APPLAUSE

Kathy Fish

| | | |

Acknowledgments

"The Next Stanley Kubrick" *Monkeybicycle; Words, Words, Words*

"What Kind of Person Gives Secrets to the Sky" *Night Train*

"Shoebox" *Wild Strawberries*

"Bread" *FRiGG*

"Waterfall" *Staccato*

"How Elm Trees Die" *Pindeldyboz*

"In a School in Sioux Falls, South Dakota" *Quick Fiction*

"Lens" *Ghoti*

"Foreign Film" *Cranky*

"Delivery" *Bound Off*

"Unanimous" *Spork*

"Contained" *Gator Springs Gazette*

"Florida" *Smokelong Quarterly*

"The Hollow" *Denver Quarterly*

Table of Contents

The Next Stanley Kubrick

ONE OF THE MOST GRATIFYING ASPECTS of documenting my brother Ray's life has been my growth as a filmmaker. Some of that early stuff, when Ray was a junior and I was in eighth grade, well … it's embarrassing to watch. But one year of intense study and trial and error has made all the difference. I have, for example, watched Stanley Kubrick's *The Shining* 117 times.

My dad says Ray's got the world by the ass. He rolls his eyes to the heavens when he says it like he can't believe his good fortune. My dad sells seed corn. He has a chicken neck and shaky, useless hands. Ray's hands are golden. He plays quarterback for our undefeated high school football team. Around here, that's big time.

I taped all of Ray's football games this past fall, my dad constantly asking, "Did you get that?" The whole project had become stultifyingly boring until I experienced a creative epiphany. It occurred while taping "Ray Gets A Visit from the College Recruiter."

A man came all the way from the University of Alabama. He kept telling my mom how she didn't look old enough to have a kid in high school.

"Two kids in high school," I said, sitting on the floor.

The recruiter said, "Excuse me, darlin'."

I pointed the camera at him. "Well, now." He sipped his iced tea. "What's this?"

My dad said, "For God's sakes, Emma, leave the poor man alone and go find your brother."

Ray had excused himself after dinner. Said he'd be right back. I found him sitting on his bed leafing through a *Hustler* magazine. I flicked on the camera. Ray grinned.

It's a side-angle shot of Ray, sitting on his bed, slowly turning the pages. There's laughter from downstairs. Ray scratches his nose. He shows the naked woman with the massive breasts to the camera. Dad bursts in and yells at us to get the hell downstairs. I zoom in on his chicken neck. "Turn that damned thing off," he says, blocking the viewfinder with one trembling hand. *Finis.*

I call it, "Ray's Got The World By The Tits."

Forensics Club takes time away from learning my craft, so I quit. I watch *The Shining* in the basement and take copious notes. I go to Harlen's Cafe on Saturdays. I drink coffee and pretend it's a Starbucks. I wear a black turtleneck and my dad's old checked hat. Some of the freshman girls walk by. They point at me. They point at their heads. What is that I see in their smiles? Admiration and respect.

I have this whole library of Ray tapes my parents haven't seen. There's "Ray Pukes in the Hydrangeas" and "Ray Makes Out In the Driveway with His Best Friend's Girlfriend" and "Ray Steals a Twenty from Mom's Purse." Ray loves the secret tapes. We watch them in the basement when Mom and Dad are asleep. He sits on the couch, drinking beer and laughing. He crunches the empty cans and drops them into the paper sack at his feet.

Ray knows nothing about motif. He doesn't realize I am making a statement. Like trigonometry, the concept of irony is lost on my brother.

Over dinner, I casually throw out the question "Who's going to videotape my high school career?" This is a classic awkward moment. I wish I had the video camera. My dad pretends he didn't hear, totally focused on trying to spear a lima bean with his fork. Mom coughs.

"Joking!" I say, and they all laugh. It's pretty damned sad, but in a funny way, that there exists but one videotape of me—a shaky five-minute blurb from my fifth birthday party.

A recruiter is on his way from the Air Force Academy. I get a tight shot of Dad's hands as he attempts to straighten Ray's tie. He's telling Ray he'd better not screw this up. Mom pushes him away and fixes the knot, her back to the camera. Ray stares over her head, this hulking dark figure backlit by the sun through the picture window.

Right after graduation, Ray plans to steal Dad's car and drive all the way to California. He wants me to film his getaway. He wants to call it "Ray Fucks Up Again."

But in return he's got to take me with him. I want to go to Hollywood. I want to blow people's minds. Ray just wants to see the ocean.

What Kind of Person Gives
Secrets to the Sky?

PETER AND MEGGY AND I are putting glasses of ice water on the tables. We work in the dining room at St. Anne's Home for Aged Nuns. They wheel the Sisters in around 4:30 for their dinner so they get them back to their rooms by six. Goodnight, nuns! I stop pushing the cart and sit down. Peter asks, "What's wrong?" One of the orderlies has parked Sister William in the corner, facing the wall. "I can't stand the smell of those Harvard beets," I tell him.

My mother is dating a guy named Gil, who works for the cable company, so now we have free cable. Last night, we watched *White Oleander* and my mom kept saying, "My God, Michelle Pfeiffer is gorgeous." Finally, Gil says, "I could take or leave her." He sucks the salt off the popcorn seeds and spits them back into the bowl.

When I was little, we used to go to Shell Rock to my uncle's farm. In the spring we'd get twenty-five-cent kites and stand in the middle of an open field and give them up to the wide blue sky. My dad scribbled on a piece of paper, tore it halfway and stuck it onto the string. After a few stutters, the paper hurried away from us, up the kite string, until we couldn't see it anymore. I asked him, was that a prayer? No, he said, it was a secret.

Peter's lucky. He gets to wear a white polo shirt and khakis. Of course he looks like a dork, but consider Meggy and me in our polyester pantsuits. Harvest gold. A-line top that zips right up the middle. The pants are flared and there's piping along the sides. Once, when we went to the Barley Corn after work, I changed in the backseat of my Vega. I wadded my uniform into a ball. Two days later, I found it underneath the seat and shook it out. No wrinkles.

When my mother asked, "Who's the father?" I looked her right in the eye and said, "I don't know." I'm not stupid. What is she going to say to that?

Peter says, "no shit" and Meggy's mouth drops open. She starts to laugh. We're eating roast chicken and vanilla pudding in the break room. "Tell me what's funny because I could use a laugh," I say. "You're grossing me out, by the way." Her front teeth are coated with pudding. It's dribbling down her chin. When she can finally speak, she says, "When did this happen? I mean you're always with us. Or at school." I hand her a napkin. What Meggy doesn't seem to know is that it only takes a minute to have sex. One minute.

The Barley Corn is this dive bar we discovered in Dike. You have to drive right out of Waterloo, out into the country until you get to the little farm towns. Dike has its own Main Street and bar after bar and nobody cards. We are sophisticated. We drink sloe gin fizzes. We roll our eyes at the selections on the jukebox. You got any real music?

My mother is a large woman. She's six foot tall and she's heavy. Not fat, just big all over. And pretty. I am small, like my dad. There is nothing pretty about me. Mr. Stebbins, my algebra teacher, tells me my hair is the color of wheat and that he knows I don't dye it because most girls, if they dyed their hair, would choose a nicer shade of blonde.

I've been dreaming about monkeys. Wild monkeys attacking me, scratching and clawing at me. Gil says don't eat pizza before going to bed. But that's all there is around here anymore. And another thing, does Gil live here now?

I was in the backseat of the car. We had a big car then, with wide vinyl covered seats with springs underneath. I was bouncing on the seat and waiting for my parents to yell at me to stop, but they didn't say anything. My mother was driving. We parked at the train station and she grabbed hold of my hand. Ouch, I said. My dad got a suitcase out of the trunk and knelt down and kissed me. I asked him how come the sky was white and he said that means snow is coming. I can still see it. His sad face, the bare trees, the white sky.

I love how the guy at the Barley Corn doesn't give me any shit when I order a sloe gin fizz. I'm just having the one anyway. "Are you tired?" Peter asks. "A little." Meggy's dancing with some guy to a country song. "We could go," Peter says. Peter lost his license and now he doesn't drink anymore. I pull the maraschino cherry off the plastic sword with my teeth and swallow it. "Shall we dance?"

My dad just shows up one day. I walk in the door and there he is, sitting with my mom at the kitchen table. My dad looks about a hundred years old. I drop my book bag and kick off my shoes. "Hey," I say. He stands up and looks at me and shakes his head. Who does he think he is?

Gil wants to know what I think of the name "Gunner." To be honest; I don't think much of it at all. Gunner! My mom has no opinion. There is only so much she can think about. She keeps asking when I'm going to cash that check, the one my dad left folded and set on its ends, like a tent, on my pillow. He'd written the words, "good luck" on the memo line and underlined them. Twice.

I watched from the window as he got into his car. I thought if he waves, I'll wave back. But he only looked at me and lifted his fingers off the steering wheel, the way people do when they're just dashing out for a minute and you both know they'll be right back.

Shoebox

THEIR PARENTS WORRY ABOUT THEM because they are so thin. Their mother fries steaks, untrimmed, in butter, mashes full cream into the potatoes. They cradle spoonfuls of food on their tongues and when their father says, "chew that up and swallow it," they do, but the feel of it sliding down their throats is an agony.

They don't want to grow big and strong, they want to be left alone. They want to walk out to the open field behind their house, talk low, pluck caterpillars from the milkweed. Soon, there will be monarch butterflies the size of their mother's hands.

They get a hold of their aunt's cigarettes. They learned to read last year so they pass the pack back and forth, reading the warning label. They try to smoke the cigarettes, but their lungs are small and rigid, like stones in their chests. They lie down in the prairie grass and clutch each other, imagine dying together under fat clouds.

Their aunt comes to watch them sometimes when their parents have to go into Osage. As soon as the car disappears down the long, gravel driveway, she turns to them and says, "Go. Be One with Nature." The aunt drinks Seven & Sevens and sits on the screened porch, one hand squirming like a puppy under the blanket on her lap. Some smell rises up out of the aunt they can't identify. They are careful not to get too close.

In town, there is a school and there are other children. They know this because the aunt has told them. They sit on the floor in the far corner of the porch, staring at the ham salad sandwiches she made for them.

"You two fit inside a shoebox when you were born," the aunt says. "This big." She holds her hands up.

They have heard the story, how their mother swaddled them tightly together in one receiving blanket and their father put them in the box and took a picture. He sent it into the local newspaper. The photo ran on the front page. After that, their mother did not speak to their father—or anyone—for one full month.

They want to hear more about the town, but are afraid to ask.

"You think I care if you eat those sandwiches? I do not. I'll stuff them down the disposal and not say a word," the aunt says.

The aunt has lupus. Her face is flat and round as a paper plate. A red rash sits on the bridge of her nose and across her cheeks like a pair of reading glasses. She regards them with her little eyes.

They read the Bible and the stories their mother types up for them. The children in the stories are forever naughty and forever in peril. In the end, the children repent and all is well. Still, God looms over their shoulders as they play, disappointed and angry.

They press their palms over a triangle of sunlight on the edge of the blanket. A truck rattles past on the road behind the stand of evergreen trees. Both girls turn their heads and listen hard.

Bread

ZACH IS FIXING US HIS FAMOUS fisherman's omelets and fried potatoes. The omelets are filled with mushrooms and crabmeat and whitefish and scallions and the smell of them cooking in butter is making me swoon. And we are, let's face it, a little drunk already. We're all in town, the siblings, for the first time in two years.

Zach slides an omelet onto a plate and piles potatoes over the top of it and hands it to me. "Eat up. You could use a few pounds."

My brother Rob is already chowing down. He pats his belly. "Contentment," he says, like he always does. I pull a chair up next to him.

"I work out is all." I shake the ketchup bottle over my potatoes and it comes out all at once. I mix it all together with my fork.

"That is truly disgusting," Rob says and for a second I think he's referring to my working out.

Zach sits down with his own plate. A beam of sunlight hits the top of his bald head, like a penlight flicking on. Ted, our other brother, the one whose son has died, is at his house with his wife. The movers are coming tomorrow; they've decided to go ahead with the move to Santa Fe.

"Remember Mom used to make creamed eggs on toast? Does anybody make that anymore?" Rob's talking around his food.

"Creamed eggs on toast is a poor people food," I say. We also used to have bread and gravy for dinner; we all remember this, though our mother denied ever having given us a dinner that lacked essential protein.

Zach lifts his glass. "Look at us! We eat like kings. Kings!"

Rob and I lift our glasses, too, and we're laughing hard. Nothing's funny really. Zach looks at the clock.

"We'd better hustle. We're supposed to be there by 10:30," he's saying this to Rob. They're to be the pallbearers. We all go quiet, like we've been switched off.

Rob pushes his plate away. He's messing around with his napkin, folding it and unfolding it. He leans over and covers his face with his hands. "I still can't fucking believe this," he says. I pat my brother's broad back. He's sobbing and I can't even work up one tear. I don't want to go to the funeral. I don't want to see my brother grieving. Or my sister-in-law. I don't want to see my nephew in a casket. The last time I saw him I gave him some of my pot, teased him about his girlfriend. I drink the last of my Bloody Mary. The phone is ringing.

Waterfall

I'M TAKING A WATERFALL TO MY DAD. One of those things you set on your desk and plug in. Supposed to be very soothing. It's a going away present even though I'm the one who's going away. Dad lives in a retirement home right behind the Home Depot and the nicest thing about the place is the large bird cage in the foyer. It's very ornate.

My friend, Judy, and I are partners in a catering business we call "The Good Egg." One of our chief aims is to bring devilled eggs back to the level of popularity they enjoyed in the 50s and 60s. We're expanding, opening a new store in Denver because Judy likes mountains. She wants to go see my dad, too.

My daughter, Eleanor, comes along too, but she doesn't like it much. She stays in the foyer with the birds and the old folks parked in their wheelchairs. She finds them very companionable. The birds have plenty of room to fly around. It can make you dizzy if you watch them too long.

Dad's watching a fight on cable. They've got him propped up in his chair. His room smells like its only purpose for the past hundred years has been to cook tapioca.

"Jesus!" He looks at Judy and me and then back at the TV. "This guy's getting the living shit beat out of him."

That cracks Judy up. She pats Dad on the shoulder. "Hello to you, too, Mr. Randall."

I'm delighted though. It's the longest string of words I've heard out of him in awhile. I set the waterfall on his desk. I'll let the nurse mess with it later.

"We're just about set, Dad. Leaving for the Mile High City tomorrow. Can I have a butterscotch?" I ask and take one from the bowl. "Yep. As you can see, I'm pretty nervous."

We pull up chairs and watch the fight with him. There's a photo of a young woman taped to the corner of the TV. She's wearing a cap and gown. There is a gap in her front teeth.

"So. Who's that?" I ask, but I guess Dad is done talking for today.

Judy finds a six pack of Bud in his little fridge. "Want one?" She asks me.

"I wonder who's buying him that."

Judy drinks the beer and sits on Dad's bed, flipping through his photo album from his Navy days. "Man, you were sharp looking, Mr. Randall," she says. "Mmm, mmm."

"Yeah, he was. Like Gregory Peck." I see he's fallen asleep so I get up and kiss his bald head and we go.

The birds are making a hell of a racket. We find Eleanor standing next to one of the residents, sticking her index finger into his ear.

"What? He likes it," she says and the old guy nods. Yes, yes, it's true.

This Is Dwight

RON AND BETHAL ARRIVE WITH THEIR SON. Ron hands me a gift. Two beeswax candles tied with a bow that looks like straw.

"This is Dwight."

I shake the boy's hand. "Is that you I've heard whistling in the mornings? You're a champion."

Bethal looks around. "It's roomy. I've never been inside this place."

I've invited them for nachos and margaritas. I invited everyone on the street, but they were the only ones who could make it. I am, by God, never moving again.

"I've made limeade for you," I tell Dwight. "You can have it in one of my margarita glasses. See, the stems are shaped like cacti."

"Oh, the kitchen is tiny, though," Bethal says. She takes a seat at the counter. I still have boxes everywhere.

"Dwight is always cheerful," says Ron. "Whistle something for us, buddy."

"Wait just a sec." I give the margaritas another zip in the blender and pour out one for each of us.

Dwight takes a sip of his limeade and sets down his glass. His father and mother are looking at him. His eyes are cast down, as if he's composing himself. I start to say he doesn't have to if he doesn't want to, but Bethal says, "Shh."

Dwight lifts his head and stares straight ahead and whistles "Red River Valley." When he finishes, Ron and Bethal clap, so I clap too.

"Wow. That was so sad sounding. So...melodious. Is that the word?"

Bethal sips her margarita. "Dwight attends a Steiner school. The children are not taught to read until they have lost all their milk teeth."

"Bravo," I say. "My mother says I didn't learn to tie my shoes until I was nine years old. And look at me now!"

I carry the plate of nachos out onto the deck and the three of them follow me. I want to tell them I have a little boy too and that he may come to visit sometimes, but I'm not sure. I don't want to jinx it.

"It's a good neighborhood," Ron says, looking around. "Everyone's clean and quiet, but friendly."

"They're only friendly when they need you. You'll see." Bethal raises her glass as if she's made a toast.

"Really, now. Bethal sometimes makes her points too strenuously. It's because she's so passionate."

"Well, no. That's not it," she says. Bethal's eyelids droop, like clay that's softened. I want to put my thumbs on them and push up. I hope my face doesn't look as sad as hers.

"What grade are you in, Dwight? Do you play soccer?" I top off Ron and Bethal's drinks and my own. "Seems like all kids play soccer these days."

"Dwight made those candles we gave you," Ron says. "Didn't you, buddy?"

"But I want to hear about you," Bethal says. "Where are you from? I can't place your accent."

"I'm from Nebraska. Nebraskans have an unplaceable accent. It's like—everything and nothing at the same time."

Ron laughs. "That's marvelous!" He scoops up a nacho and pops it into his mouth.

"I've lived lots of places though."

Bethal takes Ron's hand and squeezes it. I wait for them to ask me about the places I have lived, but they don't.

Dwight has jumped up onto the deck railing. His legs are white and hairless. His tee shirt says, "Number One Rocker." It appears to have been pressed. I smell barbecue, hear people laughing. The sun is dropping behind the mountains.

"Well…" Bethal says and she and Ron stand up.

"You don't have to leave."

Then Dwight starts to tell me about his new travel pillow. He got it at a camping supply store and it can be stuffed into a pouch no bigger than a field mouse.

"Did you know the pillow is the single most important item to ensure a traveler's comfort?" Dwight asks. Bethal says, "Shh," but I tell her no, let him talk; I like the sound of his voice.

How Elm Trees Die

THIS IS MY DAD AT THE BREAKFAST TABLE. He's leaning towards my brother, Den, like he's telling him some wild secret except his voice is plenty loud enough for Mom and me to hear. Den has asked Dad to explain why all the trees in town are dying.

Dad says that when the hot wind blows it gets the trees swaying and whispering to each other. "That's all it is, boy. Trees gossiping, spreading disease." He smiles at Mom. "Isn't that right, baby?" He used to call her Constance, but this summer he has started calling her "baby." I don't know why.

And this is my mom. She's got a paisley kerchief wrapped around a head full of pink curlers and she's wearing lipstick even though it is only breakfast. She drinks black coffee from a green mug that shows a leaping deer and the words "Nothing runs like a Deere" on it.

"Aren't you the poet this morning, Ray!" She laughs. I swear I smell the scent of Tide out her red mouth. "Whispering trees, that's sweet. Really."

I can't eat for the whine of chain saws. We've got a hundred-year old elm tree of our own right outside our house. There's an archway of elm trees that blocks the sky the whole length of our street. The chain saws sound like they are three, maybe four blocks away.

Den has stopped listening. He's scooping forkfuls of scrambled eggs like yellow brains into his mouth. He is twelve, two years older than I am.

Dad's working his teeth over with a pick, watching Mom.

"Gossip kills, doesn't it baby?" Something about his voice makes me feel dizzy. I grip the edge of my chair.

Mom's looking at the paper. Just looking at it. Dad gets up to leave.

"Don't trip over your lunch pail, Poet," she says.

Around town, cut logs lay scattered like bones. Den and his friends like to walk Indian style across the logs, one foot in front of the other, stretching their arms out at their sides for balance. I sit watching them in the shadow of our school. The new, huge sky wants to swallow me. I try not to look at it. I like the feel of concrete beneath me, of bricks against my back.

A man is singing "C'mon baby light my fire" over my transistor radio. I turn up the volume and push my bangs off my forehead. The boys are playing follow-the-leader now. Den calls over his shoulder we'll go home in five minutes. I focus my attention on his sneakers flying over the dead limbs.

I don't tell Den anything anymore. Not since I let it slip that I had had some troubles with gravity and he'd gone straight to Mom and told her. She felt my forehead and wanted me to explain, but how could I? It was the day Sister William stood Leonard Tucker up at the front of the class for blowing raspberries during "The Battle Hymn of the Republic." She asked him to recite the Five Glorious Mysteries and when he couldn't (she knew he couldn't) she whacked him on the back of his head with those toady hands of hers. I had felt suddenly lighter and next thing I knew I was watching Leonard Tucker and Sister William from somewhere near the ceiling. I saw myself, too, at my desk, holding my songbook out in front of me like everyone else.

Dad had come into my room after work smelling like the hot metal shavings under his skin and explained to me all about Gravity like a Poet, which meant I didn't understand a single word. I knew that Gravity did not "hug me close to Mother Earth" all the time as apparently it did everyone else. I nodded to make him smile, but I learned after that to curl my toes in tightly when I walked and to sit heavily in chairs.

On Mullan Avenue, it is cooler and darker. I scan the trees overhead. Look to the tallest branches and see a scattering of brown leaves near the top of several of the trees. I drop down at the foot of the elm tree that stands in front of our house. I see my mom through the windows of the house, moving about her work, her hair still in curlers. The scent of Tide blows out the dryer vent and rises and blends with the hot breeze. The tops of the trees begin to sway and whisper, "Your mother, your mother, your mother…" but I don't know what they are trying to tell me.

Soon, my dad appears around the corner swinging his lunch pail. His face is long. I decide not to run to him. I press my bottom hard to the ground beneath our elm tree. The men with the chain saws will come soon. I will wait for them.

In a School in Sioux Falls, SD

A GIRL HAS BEEN SENT to the cloak room for eating glue. She can't help herself, she is compelled. She has fallen in love with the benevolent, smiling cow on the label. Dried glue on her fingertips makes her think of peeling skin and summers on some beach. Out the tall, narrow window snow stretches to the highway like a thin, white plate. The girl pulls all the coats and snowsuits off their hooks. She piles them into a mound and crawls inside. She is known as the fidgeter. She has a monopoly on demerits. If one more cross is chalked up after her name she will surely hang. The children sing a song about Christ. She buries herself in deeper.

Lens

PRUE WAS A SCARECROW OF A WOMAN, thin and hard with a straight mouth. But she knew the secret for growing tulips. Her tulips were bright yellow and blood-red, eighteen inches tall in full bloom. Their heads swung round in the Kansas breeze. She worked for the county and lived alone.

A photographer came from the *Wichita Eagle*.

"Well, there they are," she said, pointing.

He laughed. "No, I want you, too." He made her lie flat on her stomach in the grass, her face level with the blooms. "They're exquisite," he said. "How do you do it?"

"Do you know," she said, "that strangers come round to see my flowers? Little girls in Easter bonnets trample my garden. They pick my flowers and don't ask permission."

His elbows planted in the dirt, he aimed the camera and adjusted the lens, took pictures until the sun sank low.

They entered her house through the kitchen door. The photographer unbuttoned her long cotton shirt, pulled down her loose pants. He touched her grim mouth with the tips of his fingers, ran his hands down her slim, hard body. In bed, she was silent when the photographer cried out.

Night fell and the photographer slept, one hand between Prue's legs. She lay awake and watched the light from passing cars travel the walls of her bedroom, then disappear.

Foreign Film

THEY ARE WATCHING A MOVIE about a man who cheats on his wife, whom he loves, and is so disconsolate that his wife eventually loses all patience and leaves him. They are at the point in the film where the man considers his many blunders as he walks along a rocky shoreline carrying what looks to be a large vase. The director of the film is Yugoslavian.

They have argued through dinner and through the night and now it's nearly dawn. They have no eyes for subtitles. The musical score unnerves them. It is exactly the sound of an accordion squeezing the life out of a kitten.

The woman rolls off the couch and lies on the floor. The light in the room changes. Through the window, the clouds resemble dove's feathers. The man stretches his legs out. He mutes the television and chuckles. She thinks he muted the television to make sure she would hear him chuckle.

"I'm going out there," she says, pointing. "I'm going to put my boots on and go for a walk."

The disconsolate man's face fills the screen but the couple is no longer watching. The subtitles flash in quick succession.

"And when I get back, I'm taking a shower," she continues. "And you, Laughing Man, you can do whatever you want."

The man in the film stares. The screen is clear of words. His gaze is urgent and equable.

"Are you listening to me?" she asks. She has not gotten up. She has not put on her boots.

"It's all here," he says, tapping his forehead. "It's been archived." He chuckles again, eyes closed.

The room brightens. She stands and hovers over him. He is sleeping. She splays the fingers of one hand and lowers them to his face. The click and whoosh of the furnace makes her jump. She turns to the television. The disconsolate man has waded into the surf. He cocks the vase back in his palm and heaves it in a wide arc into the sea.

Delivery

THE DOORBELL RANG. It was an older gentleman wearing a tuxedo, a bundle in his arms.

"Here," he said, handing it over.

"It's a baby," Mabel said. Its wee mouth gaped, emitting an odd, churring sound, like a hummingbird.

The man smiled. "A newborn," he said.

She held the bundle out in front of her. The swaddling came loose. The infant burped. "I was expecting a vintage radio. I didn't order this."

"We had to make a substitution."

"I don't even like babies. The whole motherhood thing..." Mabel shuddered.

"And yet..."

The thing was unwieldy. Mabel held it out to the man. It slipped out of its blankets and fell to the floor.

Mabel and the tuxedoed gentleman stared. The infant yowled.

"Are you going to pick it up?" Mabel asked.

"I don't think so." The man clasped his hands behind his back, yawed to the right and to the left like a metronome. The infant screamed. Mrs. Yeardley, Mabel's next door neighbor, stared from the sidewalk. Her annoying little dog, Huntley, yapped.

"Is there a problem?" Mrs. Yeardley called, but got no response.

"Oh for God's sake," Mabel said. She picked up the baby and hoisted it over her shoulder. "This is obviously a mistake."

"I'm very good with babies," Mrs. Yeardley called, a little louder. The man turned and held his hand up to her.

"All's well here," he said. "Just a little adjustment phase. It's quite normal. Go on about your business."

Mabel patted the infant on the bottom, bounced on her knees, swung from side to side. Still, it cried, its damp cheek against her own. The man in the tuxedo was saying something but it was difficult to make out.

"I should get a what? A nine-volt battery? Is that what you said? Come back here!"

The man was already down the steps and unlatching the gate. He turned and smiled. "Well," he said. "Enjoy."

The infant settled lumpily against Mabel's breast. "You smell like oatmeal," Mabel said. She pinched its nose and twisted it. "You are not a vintage radio. Not even close."

Laughter, Applause. Laughter, Music, Applause

THE LADY ACROSS THE STREET was pregnant. She came over with a pie and pinned a clean diaper on my baby brother and asked where are your parents? Grandmother came in the back door and thanked the lady and asked her to leave. Grandmother's hair was up in curlers with papers in them. They reminded me of the egg rolls at China King. She tidied things up a little though there was nothing much to tidy up and ran a bath and hustled down to the Laundromat to call the hospital on the pay phone.

In the afternoon, the younger ones started to cry and she sat cross-legged on the floor and told them a story about a duck family who lived on a pond of India ink and the ducks, when they waddled out, made prints all up and down the city streets. The little ones yawned and she lay down with them on a quilt on the floor. I sat on the step wanting our old house and wanting mother.

A crow got into the house through the attic window and flew into the window glass and dropped to the floor. Grandmother heard and got up and got the broom, told me to hold the door open and she swatted it out of the house, cussing and swearing. Grandmother mowed the lawn then and took me over with her to the lady's to thank her for the pie and to apologize for being rude before. She asked the lady if she could watch us kids for awhile as she had to go to the hospital and visit our mother and here, she dropped her eyes and the lady felt sorry for us and came back over and told Grandmother to take her time. The lady leaned against the wall, holding her back. She wore a silk robe with primroses on it and tiny slippers. She told us be good and go straight to bed even though it was still light out. I told my brothers we should do like she said and we went up and lay on the floor, listening to *Comedy Hour* coming through the windows of the house next door.

Prodigy

I USED TO BE ABLE to do multi-digit multiplication in my head. When I was seven, my dad woke me up in the middle of the night and drove me three hours to Sioux City to show this guy what I could do. The guy came out onto his lawn, stood with one hand on his hip, kinda womanly. My dad said, "I want you to see this." The guy spit something into the grass. We stood on that guy's dead grass, my dad firing multi-digit multiplication problems at me and me answering until my teeth were chattering and I had to pee. Finally my dad said, "Okay? Okay?" The guy turned and walked back to his house. "Okay," he said.

Unanimous

THE MIME WAS ALWAYS ON and though he was very good, it was annoying because it forced you to always look at him. If you had him over for dinner, say, and you were chopping parsley or grinding spices or peeling an orange and you asked him a question, something simple like, Did you enjoy the movie *Crash?*, you would have to lay down your knife or your pestle or your orange and watch The Mime give his answer. In this case, it was fingers thrust through hair, eyes rolling back in the head, a rocking from side to side, a gaping of the mouth. There was no multi-tasking when The Mime was around. And you'd go to sleep later and the whole evening was an endless movie reel starring The Mime. We had an Oscar party and decided, collectively, not to invite The Mime. We invited an opera singer instead. A woman we'd met only the week before. We felt fickle doing this, but really.

Contained

HEFFERMAN AVOIDED BEAUTIFUL WOMEN. They were fussy, he reasoned, and vain and disloyal. Relationships were hard. Margaret was not a beautiful woman, nor was she ugly. For the moment, she was his supervisor.

He worked as an indexer. Margaret edited his printouts with a scratchy felt tipped pen, writing comments like "Freud, yes! Psychoanalysis, no!" Sometimes she drew faces next to her comments. Eyes, nose and a frustrated, squiggled up mouth. Hefferman was charmed. His were the only printouts with faces on them.

He stirred his coffee and peeked around the wall of his cubicle. He didn't see her fingers clicking over the keyboard or the wisp of steam rising from her daily latte. He didn't see her startling, slim legs.

A package sat on her desk, wrapped in shiny paper and atop it, the spray of cherry blossoms he had clipped from the tree outside the building. The security guard glared at him, but Hefferman shook his head and laughed. "Don't prosecute me, sir. I am in love!" He was sure that, deep down, the security guard was a kind and reasonable man.

At last he heard the gasp of Margaret's Nikes as she moved down the hall. She slumped into her chair. Hefferman waited. He patted his cheeks. They were warm. He expected, but didn't hear, the womanly cry of joy at discovering a gift. What he heard was more akin to a moan. He crossed over to Margaret's cubicle.

"Margaret?"

She rubbed her forehead. She had kicked off the Nikes, but not yet replaced them with pumps. Her feet, in pantyhose, smelled of sweat and petroleum product.

"Another migraine?" He asked.

She rocked forward and got up. Hefferman stood eye level to her shoulders. "I'll be in the bunker," she said.

Shoved into one corner of the conference room sat a refrigerator carton, which contained a silk blanket and a pillow filled with dried lavender. On headache days, Margaret would climb inside and wait out the pain like an injured cat.

"Don't worry about a thing!" Hefferman called down the hall to her. "I shall hold down the fort while you rest."

For the next hour, he popped around from cubicle to cubicle, talking to the other indexers.

"Margaret's in the bunker, okay? Any questions or problems, direct them to me."

"Oh, for sure! Jeez, you crack me up, Hefferman." This, from the 23 year-old who had admittedly worked in indexing for two years, as opposed to Hefferman's three months. But did he have to remind her that he had six hours of postgraduate credits under his belt?

Already, the cherry blossoms on Margaret's gift had turned brown around the edges. Hefferman took the package to the conference room and got down on his knees and squinted into the opening of the refrigerator box. She was snoring.

He jiggled her ankle. She didn't respond. He jiggled harder. She pushed up on her elbows. Her eyes were slits, her jaw gaped.

"I just wanted to report that I've got everything under control," he said.

"Under control? What happened?"

"I just mean that I've apprised the other employees of the situation."

"Well, good."

"And I brought you something."

Hefferman set the box on the mound of Margaret's stomach. She didn't touch it.

"It's not my birthday."

"Do I need an excuse? Go ahead. Open it."

"This isn't really appropriate. I thought we spoke about this. Here," she said, pushing the parcel into Hefferman's hands. "I'm going back to sleep."

"No! I mean. Ha! Listen to us, Margaret. Bickering like an old married couple." He brushed her knee with his hand.

"Do I need to call security?"

He couldn't believe his ears. Were these words inevitable, then? Were all women insane?

She sunk her head in her hands and groaned. "I really don't need this right now," she said.

"Tell me what you do need, then. Tell me anything." The scent of lavender and Margaret suffocated him. His knees hurt. She wasn't a beautiful woman, but she was reasonable, he was certain of that.

Hefferman pulled a pen from his shirt pocket and drew a face on the package. Eyes, nose and a frustrated, squiggled up mouth. He reached in for Margaret's hand and placed the gift on her palm. She looked at it and shook her head, tore off the cherry blossoms, now limp, and slowly removed the wrapping.

Florida

EVERY MORNING SHE CHANGES out of her wet nightgown and goes into the bathroom and shakes her mother's Cashmere Bouquet talcum powder all over her body and into a fresh pair of underpants before she dresses for school. For about an hour she smells like perfume. Once, she saw her dad put Ban roll-on on his armpits and then swipe a big "X" of it across his chest. She tried this, but the kids at school said Ban roll-on smells worse than piss.

She asks her mother if she can take a bath in the mornings. "But how will you ever learn if you don't suffer the consequences?" Her mother says, pointing to her chin. "You have cereal there."

"So be it," Emmeline says.

Dick Fencl draws pictures of army planes and war scenes during class. At recess, he stands inside the monkey bars and sings "The Ballad of the Green Berets." He and Emmeline are both on the chunky side. They don't climb the monkey bars and everybody leaves them alone there. Emmeline wishes Dick Fencl would sing something a little more up-tempo.

They're getting their history papers back today. They were supposed to write a biography about a person from Civil War Times. She was going to write about Abraham Lincoln but then found a book about his wife, Mary Todd Lincoln.

Mary Todd Lincoln reminds her of her Aunt Janine, who takes off every few months and drives to Florida and Emmeline's mom and grandma have to track her down and commit her. When she's not being committed, though, she's okay. She paints Emmeline's toenails and gives her sips of the cocktails she learned to make tending bar at Vic's Tavern. In her paper, Emmeline compares Mary Todd Lincoln's crazy, which involved spending lots of money and going to séances, with her Aunt Janine's, which involves wearing cowgirl outfits and running with strange men.

So all the kids get their papers back except Emmeline. Sister Valeria calls her up.

"This," she says, flapping the paper on her desk, "is filth and nonsense." She's glaring at her. Behind her, Pope Paul and President Nixon are glaring at her too.

Emmeline wants to say, "So be it" but she can't open her mouth. She's sweating in her wool jumper (with the embroidered heart for the Sacred Heart of Jesus) and that stink melds with her usual, pissy smell. Sister Valeria wrinkles up her nose and tears up the paper on Mary Todd Lincoln and orders her to write another one, twice as long. Emmeline is ordered to kneel in the back of the room and say a rosary. Out loud.

The floor hurts her knees. The kids are turning around in their seats to look at her. Dick Fencl is smiling goofily, giving her the thumbs up.

If she closes her eyes and breathes deep enough, she finds she doesn't smell so bad.

blessedisthefruitofthywooomJesus The words make her feel like she's all alone in a shiny new place. She wonders if Dick Fencl feels like this when he's singing about the Green Berets. Nowandatthehourofourdeathamen

Mary Todd Lincoln was holding her husband's hand when he was shot in the back of the head at Ford's Theater. After the funeral, she holed up in the White House for six weeks and then one day she put on a fancy black dress and went to Chicago. Like that.

The Hollow

AFTERNOONS, THE GIRLS PLAY IN THE HOLLOW. The heat buckles their energy and sweat drips into their eyes. Their mother works hard, but the girls are unkempt and secretive, given to a layered, sarcastic wit.

Their mother bakes olive bread and cinnamon rolls. She is never cross, but occasionally she has quiet days where she doesn't speak to the girls. It is as if her head is wrapped in gauze with two holes for her eyes.

The school is two miles away and the girls walk. In this day and age! It is a matter of pride for the mother that the girls walk to school, rain or shine. "We can do anything," she tells them. "There is nothing we can't do!"

They live on the edge of town. There is a cornfield behind their house. When the wind blows, it is like the hands of many children clapping.

Their mother wears a device over her ear. It is a telephone. She walks around in public places, talking and gesturing, sometimes swearing. The girls are frightened because their mother looks like a crazy person. She will look at them and say, "What? What are you staring at?"

The woman at True Value Hardware has pigtails and a hunched, contemplative posture. She asks, "What is the nature of your problem?"

The girls spin and jump. The nature of their problem! They want to take the woman in the blue apron behind the doors with the sign that says "Authorized Personnel Only" and tell her everything. That their mother sits in the garage when she gets home and leaves the car running and she cranks 101.7 The Rock and closes the garage door. The girls are young, but they are not stupid. They run down the stairs and push the garage door opener. Their mother reclines in the driver's seat. She sings along with her eyes closed. She doesn't hear the garage door open. When the song is over, she opens her eyes and is annoyed. "Why are you up? Get back to bed." But then she comes in and lets them pull off her shoes, she lets them put rainbow clips in her hair. She lets them watch *Unsolved Mysteries* until she falls asleep on the couch.

But their mother answers the woman, "My door has come off its hinges," and she shows her the broken hinge, the stripped screws.

The mother has started a home business, selling her goods to local grocery stores. She puts on black polyester pants, kitten heels and a tailored blouse. She has frosted her hair. The girls do not like the way her bottom looks in the pants, like the thorax of an ant. They don't like her striped hair.

She talks to suppliers on the phone. She needs plastic bags and paper trays for the cinnamon rolls. She needs only plastic bags for the olive bread. Both require labels. The mother has designed the labels herself, working late at night on her computer. She calls her products "Goodness Gracious," which the girls think is dumb. Behind her back, they say, "Goodness gracious, this is awful!" and "Goodness gracious, I'm going to puke!"

The labels feature a smiling sun. The girls think they could draw a better one, but the mother says they don't appreciate her primitive style. The mother thinks this is hilarious. They do not want the olive bread or the cinnamon rolls. They ask for Kraft macaroni and cheese. They want Kids' Cuisine.

Their father has a new apartment he has furnished lavishly with Norwegian style furniture. The girls think it looks like a doctor's office with the magazines fanned out on the coffee table. The rooms smell like toothpaste.

He takes them to the place he used to work. He paces around outside the building. They struggle to keep up. There are windows, but they can't see inside. He turns and says, "Does anybody have to wee?"

He rushes them through the revolving door. The security guard puts up his hand. "You've been told," he says. He's a giant, taller and wider than their father.

"Hey, man, my daughters have to pee." The security guard looks at the girls and shakes his head. "Sorry kids," he says. Their father sits outside on a cement bench, smoking, while the girls chase each other around the topiary.

He drops them home and there's soup in the crockpot, bubbling over. The floor is slick with flour. The girls sweep and wipe and eat from bowls on the back porch. They catapult navy beans into the grass. "Fine dining, fine dining!" they cry.

Later, they are woken by laughter. The girls tumble from their beds and look out the window. It is their mother, beyond the hollow on the edge of the cornfield in the blue night, her arms wild, waving down the moon.

About the Author

Kathy Fish has published over eighty stories both online and in print. Recent work is published or is forthcoming in *Quick Fiction, Smokelong Quarterly, Night Train, Spork, [sic] literary journal, Denver Quarterly, FRiGG, Storyglossia, New South* and elsewhere. Four of her stories have been nominated for the Pushcart Prize.

WANTING

Amy L. Clark

| | | |

Acknowledgments

"Wanting" *Fringe*

"Things I have wanted to be when I grow up" *Louis Liard*

"Dear Mr. President" *McSweeney's Internet Tendency; Brevity & Echo: An Anthology of Short Short Stories*

"How to Burn a House" *Quick Fiction; Brevity & Echo: An Anthology of Short Short Stories*

Table of Contents

Measurements

WE DIDN'T GET HOME until after ten at night. During the ride back from the airport, when I wasn't praying that my husband would stay awake at the wheel, I had been thinking about curling up in bed with a magazine and falling asleep with my reading glasses still on. But when we got home it turned out the dog was dead. Cletus was an old dog, and there he was lying out on the cold hearth of the fireplace we never used and not moving.

We came upon the dog at the same moment, and for this I was glad. The first thing I thought when I saw Cletus like that was that I was lucky I didn't have to tell my husband what had happened. Facts are always easier than words. And nothing I could have said would have sounded right in my mouth. I have made no secret of the fact that I have always hated that dog, and I absolutely loathe speaking the name Cletus. But Cletus has lived with my husband longer than I have, and there is probably more knowledge of the man in one dead, flea-bitten ear than I will ever have.

My husband is not the type to cry. But standing there, his head sort of drooped down to his chest. Then he turned around and left the room and it was just me and Cletus in the gloom. I thought about Cletus's big tongue licking me when I first moved in here, and my husband filling the bathtub with tomato juice and plopping Cletus in that time he got sprayed by a skunk. The kids across the street had been feeding Cletus this weekend and he must have been fine this morning when they walked him because they had our number. Cletus was, it is true, an old dog. And then, I couldn't help it, I thought of the luggage in the car that needed still to be unloaded and put away.

My husband, who is a physicist, came back into the living room with something dangling from his fist. We had been at a weekend conference on neutrinos, which I will never understand. But I had gone along because it was a free ticket to California, even if it was only Fresno, and he and I are trying to do things together. My husband went over to Cletus and started stroking his muzzle, but he stopped quickly. Dead dogs are not like dogs when they are alive. Then he wedged his forearms under Cletus and lifted him up. Cletus was a lab, and not a small dog. He was stiff, too, and that made him seem bigger than when he was alive. My husband almost dropped him at first. But he carried him awkwardly to the door, with his head sticking out at an unnatural angle. I trailed along behind their odd shadow.

When we got out to the edge of the backyard, by the tool shed, I realized what my husband had in his hand. It was his tool belt and his headlamp. He strapped the lamp to his forehead and switched it on. There was a little pool of light now on the dog's face, until my husband turned away. He looked so ridiculous with that thing on his head that I almost laughed. Then he pulled his measuring tape off his tool belt. I watched him measure Cletus and make the appropriate marks on the ground. Suddenly I felt an enormous surge of what I can almost call tenderness for any man who has ever measured a dog.

My husband went into the tool shed then, and I could hear him moving things around by the light of his idiotic lamp. I shivered a little in the night. I heard him mutter. "Where," he called, "is the shovel?" His voice rose and broke on the word shovel. I didn't say that I knew exactly where the shovel was. I had leant the shovel to our neighbor a month ago, when he was planting a tree in his backyard. I had loaned a lot of things to our neighbor recently, which my husband knew and wasn't saying. That was part of the reason I was in Fresno learning about neutrinos, which I will never understand.

He came out of the shed with a little gardening spade. The one I had used to weed out around the geraniums last month. I watched him start digging, next to Cletus and exactly between the marks he had made. He threw the dirt into a neat pile beside him. Cletus would have loved tracking all that dirt into the house. It took my husband forever with the spade. I stood there the whole time, because it seemed like the thing to do. And sometime after one in the morning I thought that this must be what is meaningful. Standing there all night while a person buries something important in the backyard.

Baked Stuffed

IT'S HALFWAY THROUGH MY SHIFT, and normally I'd be in the walk-in with the bags of frozen calamari doing whip-its from the empty whipped cream bottles. Actually, Rusty taught me a way to do them with the full ones too, if you're careful. But the head chef, whose boyfriend recently lost his left foot in a motorcycle accident, has taken to sitting in the walk-in drinking coffee brandy and mumbling about how he just can't pull the legs off the lobsters anymore. If he keeps up that lobster bullshit Dmitri will fire him for sure.

So what I'm doing now is, I'm sitting on the tank of the toilet in one of the stalls in the men's room sniffing some beautiful white Rusty gave me at an introductory rate. Rusty sells all sorts of stuff, and he's pretty good about letting us sample it first, and he's even better about giving the busboys and the dishwashers a break on the price. Rusty says that way, even though he's a waiter and wears a tie, we'll remember him when the revolution comes.

I'm snorting it right off the back of my hand, and it's good. It's really good, so when it's gone I sit for a minute in the restroom imagining a scene, which is better than thinking of butter rolls all night. And this is the scene: A husband and wife are meeting in our restaurant to finalize the terms of their impending divorce. It doesn't take a whole lot of imagination to conjure this up actually, because I'm pretty sure that's a husband and wife, no kids, early thirties, not too fashionable, Jews I think, who are sitting out there at table three finalizing their divorce. If I ever get married and then get divorced I will make sure to meet somewhere a little less tacky to hash out the details. Somewhere with white tablecloths and no gingham anywhere.

Anyway, I'm sitting in the stall thinking about this couple and how it's still amazing to me that if two people are sitting there drinking their wine and a waiter comes to bring their clams casino or their lazy lobster or one of those little salads with exactly four croutons on top like the points on a compass, the couple will immediately stop talking, like it would be immodest to allow the waiter to hear what they're saying to each other. But if a busboy comes to clear the four-top next to theirs, or even to refill their own water glasses, the conversation just keeps on coming like they can't even see me, or like I probably can't understand English, being a busboy and all.

So when I was out on the floor last, bringing them their second basket of rolls, they didn't even lower their voices. And the wife said, "The dog never liked me anyway. I could never figure out whose fault that was: mine, or the dog's, or yours. I suppose it doesn't matter." He's wearing a wedding ring, she's not. In between sentences, she's eating rolls like they're the children she never had.

I lean my head back against the cool tile and tap another modest sniff onto the webbed part between my thumb and my index finger. Another blow and I'm imagining telling my girlfriend Justine about the couple at table three when I get home tonight. I know just what Justine will say. She'll say she bets the guy was a fat bastard, which he isn't. And she'll say she hopes he paid for the whole meal, and that if she were the woman at table three she would have ordered the most expensive thing on the menu. Then I'll ask Justine if she knows what the most expensive thing on the menu is, and she'll say it's the calamari, which it isn't. Justine will say she bets the couple was terrible tippers and that she can just imagine the guy's sad-sack plastic wallet flopped on the table. She'll say the guy probably downed more than his share of T and Ts during the meal and that she bets the wife asked for the I Can't Believe It's Not Butter. And I won't tell Justine that she's wrong. I won't say a goddamned thing.

Out at table three they should have just had the plates set down in front of them. The way Rusty does it, people look at their meals like he's just given them what they never knew they always wanted.

But in the stall with a buzz in the back of my throat, sur- rounded by porcelain and feeling like all the light bouncing off the tiles is being sucked right into my pupils, I'm imagining the chandelier above this husband and wife in the dining room. Popping one bulb, and then another. That shoddy brass chan- delier with the bulbs made to look like the flame part of the candle. Six little flames exploding one after another, raining down tiny shards like stars, white glass falling like salt on their baked-stuffed lobsters. Like if they got married in a Jewish cer- emony and stepped on the wine glass, now it's the opposite of that. And I'll join in, throwing beer bottles from behind the bar, the pop of brown glass on their tabletop, scattered fragments all across the floor.

(For Amanda Anderson)

Looking for Nick Westlund on the MBTA

NOW THAT BOY WAS AMAZING. He was a bike messenger but he fancied himself a Picasso, and he played the cello. Twenty hours on the bus from Boston and the cello on the seat beside him. He paid for the extra ticket so the instrument wouldn't get lonely.

He was a smoker too, but not like you or I smoke. He exhaled, and then inhaled. He used to buy two packs at once, some Lucky's and some Kamels with a K and take them all out and mix them up and put them back then. So you never knew what you would get. When he moved to the Spanish section of Chicago he learned German. He hated origami, but could do a thousand paper cranes in the time it took the grass to grow. He was the one who pointed out that magic today is really just public survival, like freezing yourself in a block of ice in Times Square and emerging many days later, frostbitten and barely breathing, but alive nonetheless. Once, he showed up to work as a bike messenger wearing a tuxedo. But he always wore his helmet. He knew chess and checkers, could say mate like he meant it.

He used to watch the grass grow.

I guess if you were once a genius you are always a genius. And if you were once in Chicago you probably still are. And wouldn't that be just like him to disappear for years then show up in the phone book instead of my subway car.

Preliminary Stages
of Gum Disease

I NEVER LIE. NOT FOR YEARS. So last night, when Alex asked me, just as I was raising my vodka cranberry to my lips, what I thought of him, I told him straight out. I took a long swallow and put my drink down. And I thought for a moment and this is what I realized: Alex is a poet and also a dentist, which is romantic when you think that those are two of the four professions with the highest rate of suicide in the nation. The other two being tollbooth workers and air-traffic controllers, which is not romantic at all. I reached for my cigarette in the ashtray. Alex doesn't smoke, because he's a dentist. But sometimes, when he's drunk, he does smoke. And he's got this way of exhaling through his nose that just makes me want to knock his teeth out. And by knock his teeth out, I do not mean metaphorically. He has the whitest teeth I've ever seen, and they're big, which doesn't seem right for a poet. Plus, he talks to himself. Not out loud, but he silently moves his lips in the shape of words. Which is really funny in bars like this, where it's so loud that people are mostly just mouthing things to each other anyway. Halfway up to my mouth I realized that I didn't even want this cigarette anymore, so I brought it back to the ashtray and ground it out. Instead, I started sucking the ice out of my drink. He was still looking at me, and it occurred to me that that must be how he looks at a cavity in a tooth in the mouth of one of his patients. Sort of with sympathy and expectation but like he regrets that the mouth had to be opened and reveal all that. When I'm in his office, I stare at the overhead light. And he must be looking at my mouth just like that. Even though I am not particularly interested in the dental arts, I know that my gums bleed almost every time I brush my teeth, and that can't be good. And sitting there, in the bar, I had an almost uncontrollable urge to touch my gums, but instead I tucked my hair behind my ears with my right hand and tilted my head to look at Alex from a different angle. And then I remembered that dentists always tell you not to chew on ice because it can chip the enamel off your teeth. So that must have been why he was staring at me like that. But I wasn't going to stop chewing on the ice just because I was sitting at a bar with a dentist. If you do everything the experts tell you to, or actually, if you don't do everything they tell you not to, you will live for a very long time. And it will seem like a very long time if you can't smoke or drink or eat fried foods or chew on ice and you religiously brush for the prescribed three full minutes and then floss. Alex is only one of the many professionals I go to see on a regular basis. I have very good health insurance. But, I thought, trapping my fidgety hand between my thighs under the table, Alex is the only one I have ever ended up at a bar with after an appointment. He is the certainly the one with the biggest teeth, and the only poet. I suppose that this was why he asked me what I thought of him in the first place. He is probably banned from seeing his patients outside of the office by some oath of dental conduct. And that is romantic. But not sexy. When I think of sexy and Alex in the same sentence I think of the ADA saying: sticky, colorless film. I picked up my drink and took another sip, which was warm because I had eaten all the ice out of it, and looked at Alex again over the rim of the glass. Something of the dentist clings to Alex in any circumstance, I thought. And when I say something of the dentist, I mean the smell. Like Listerine and bubble gum fluoride paste. But actually, it's a little reassuring, because I don't want my gums to bleed. So I decided to tell him the truth. Fact: I will probably have sex with Alex. But by sex I mean straight missionary style. I'm not as kinky as you'd think. Definitely nothing with dental apparatus. And by apparatus I mean everything. Not just the picks and those sterilized little plastic vacuum cleaner tubes, but the chair too. The light in the bar was bad. I took a deep breath.

Wanting

OVER THANKSGIVING WEEKEND I sat on my father's ailing couch and held the next generation in my arms. Her name is Cassidy, and at three months her neck can support her head and she is learning how to smile. She is the first child of the new millennium that I have met personally and she belongs to my friend. Although from the way Cassidy flailed those ten tiny toes and two fat heels when her mother tried to put little yellow socks on them, I am quite sure she will belong to no one in her lifetime.

My father looked at Cassidy blowing a perfect spit bubble between her fat lips and said that sitting there, I reminded him of my mother holding me when I was tiny and perfect. I said: I am twenty-one years old. This does not remind me of anything.

My father looked a little excited and a little old; his eyebrows went up and his hands went down to his sides. In my arms Cassidy was not heavy. My father started discussing cloth diapers versus disposable with my friend. I did not say that we are doomed either way, because of chemicals in the first case or landfills in the second. But it made me think about the life span of our planet, which has had a good run, I guess. Cassidy reached for something only she could see, straining on my lap. I thought about how little time we have. The planet is heating up so quickly, and Cassidy is already three months old. By now I had wanted to buy a little baby outfit for her.

I had wanted many things, actually, though I am only twenty-one years old. I had wanted my friend to finish her education before Cassidy. I had not wanted to see the sparkle of a rock that predates her years by centuries on her left hand. Not yet. I had wanted first and foremost to slow the melting of the ice caps and speed the melting of ice around a certain organ embedded three quarters of the way up the torso, my own and other people's.

My friend was talking about Cassidy's father, how he has been working out of town for the last two months of Cassidy's three-month life, coming home only on the weekends. How even when he was home in my friend's bed there was the child crying. And when the father heard Cassidy at night he would bring Cassidy to my friend and then fall asleep again. My friend laughed at this, a short, clipped laugh. And my father laughed with her, but he gave me a look over the top of Cassidy's head that said quite clearly: not you, not now, not ever like this. I smiled at my friend in order to make her feel supported, understood, lucky, despite everything to have this light warm squirming child who was sitting in my lap making a goo noise.

I had, I will admit it only to myself, wanted Cassidy to have a different father. I had wanted Cassidy's mother not to be a mother. But in my defense, I had also wanted to be the kind of person who didn't think those things, who didn't judge. And if all that was not a possibility, I had wanted to participate in the formation of a new world where fathers at least would not have to be out of town so much to buy diapers and have health insurance.

So I snuggled Cassidy closer to my chest and looked at my father, who had changed a lot of diapers (cloth) in his day. I thought about the disaster that my generation inherited from my father's and I thought of the harm my generation will inexorably and with the best intentions enact in Cassidy's world. I was sorry that Cassidy had been born into an interval of terror, and I turned her around on my lap to face me. I whispered quietly into the six or seven wisps of hair on her head: I am sorry. I am doing the best I can and so is your mom. I will try harder to do more and want less. Learn how to smile, I said to her. Want everything.

The Day Before
Thanksgiving

SHE TOLD ME TO LIST OFF each thing I could do in less than three minutes. The list itself could take as long as needed. I could only think of complicated, unbeautiful things. Roll a cigarette, play chopsticks on the piano, crash a car.

She was the one driving, pulling past the white Ls of failing farmhouses. The radio was almost all static. On average, a pop song lasts three minutes. We were still two-hundred pop songs from her parents' house and we didn't have much to say to each other, which is the reason we were playing stupid car games. Before word games and static she had said, "My mother doesn't distrust you. It's just that she remembers everything."

Her father would want me to go hunting. Her mother would ask me to take off my shoes at the door.

I was wearing a winter jacket and four days worth of stubble. I had a coffee mug wedged between my legs, full up half with coffee and the rest of the way with vodka. I can't drink whisky because it makes me violent. I am aware of my limitations.

I asked her to list the make and model of every car she could remember ever riding in, in reverse chronological order. She said it wasn't the same. She said she asked me first.

I told her, "Hold on. Hold on." I was thinking. Say the Hail Mary, hold my breath until I pass out, make a decision.

Options for Young Women, or: what you can do other than going back to your asshole husband

Be a phlebotomist.

Become a carnie. See the world, or at least the rural parts of our country. Room and board included in your pay.

Work at a seatbelt factory.

Get breast implants, don't take care of the incisions, and sue the surgeon when they get infected.

Start your own phone-sex company.

Save money by using toilet paper for toilet paper, napkins, and paper towels.

Sell your baby to a good friend who wants one. I recommend your friend Mandy, she's good with kids.

Reinvent the drinking straw.

Train your baby to throw her voice and win *America's Got Talent*.

Open your own sweatshop.

Move in with your parents for the last time.

Take pictures.

Make a scientific discovery. Or at least print business cards with your name and the title "scientist" to hand out at job interviews.

The University of Southern Maine has a good nursing program.

Kick the can.

Create doors made of soft foam-rubber for people like the person you used to be before you left your husband. Stairs too. And the floor directly under the stairs.

Kick the can.

Become a paralegal in twelve short months. I had a friend who was a paralegal for awhile in New York City and he met this older lawyer-woman who bought him an apartment, just bought it outright. Of course, when my mother was a paralegal she had a nervous breakdown, so this could really go either way.

Become a lesbian.

Sue your husband.

Learn cable installation. You can put a car seat in that cable van and see the world, or at least the rural parts of our country.

Have a nervous breakdown.

Talk to someone who loves you. Don't stop talking until you love yourself and the person who loves you has given you a job and a place to live and childcare and some really good food.

Fight capitalism.

Go back to your asshole husband because he's probably going to be shipped out to Iraq soon anyway and come back dead.

Always Like That

"I THINK IT WAS ALWAYS LIKE THAT," he said after the bandages came off. "Or anyway, it's a nice little come-hither crook." It was less romantic when my newly bent ring finger made all my typed Ss into Ds. There were problems with plurals and of course with tense. We had only been dating for four months and we used to write love notes to each other, emails pithy and petaled, while we were both at work. He thought I was making too much of this, and told me so in a terse three lines. He had a point, "but still," I wanted to tell him, "but still," invoking instead only nonsense, or pickle herbs uttered aloud through a stuffed nose. Sometimes, lying in bed, he would put the errant finger in his mouth, closing his lips around the knuckle, as if to cut off the circulation to past harms. During working hours I thought constantly of people maimed in auto accidents or freak industrial incidents re-learning how to walk, tie their shoes, hold a fork. I wasn't adapting fast enough. My saves were anthropomorphic, even my sadness inappropriately invoked someone's father. "We have to stop talking about this," he would say at dinner or over drinks. "It's boring and unproductive." So I stopped mentioning my damage, also eliminating from conversation words containing that certain letter. The active form suffered, and my simple present. Inevitably, all the dates he and I would go on ended in d instead of s and were, therefore, in the past.

Story for Mark, Who Probably Needs Clarification

LYING ON TOP OF YOU, Mark, I decided to introduce you to the man who is recently no longer my boyfriend of long love. You didn't seem to notice that although you could throw the length and weight of my body easily off of yours, I had your head trapped between my arms, bent each at the elbow.

"How are you going to introduce me, as Next?"

I am sure that I said to you, "You're not next," and then had to clarify when you looked at me as if, I think, you were confused. "I'm not going to date you."

Which is to say that I have slept with you, was currently sleeping with you when you proposed your new name, Next, and that that is more and less than dating you. Although, even that is misleading because we have not just slept, but woken up together. What I should have said was that I do not believe in the dichotomous idea of monogamy, or generally the concept of a single soul mate. What I should have said is that I am continuously optimistic. But I didn't think that fast, and after all, there is only so much one can say.

It was a good time for you to press up against me, arching your back. Using your penis to fill in the blank, making a slow, upward statement that involved your skinny hips, instead of asking another question. And I thought about this movement and the long groan that had escaped from my lungs over the years. I think I decided then that the beating, bleeding muscle in my chest has pulsed much faster than usual in the presence of eight of those eleven, groaning momentary men and women. Pretty good, although not perfect. But who gets perfect in this world?

"Precisely," I said out loud to myself.

You wanted to know then, "How did you get this way?"

I shifted my mouth to your throat and my hand to your shaven head and ran my fingers back and forth so that I could feel what was there. "What way?"

"Very complicated and confident." Your one hand cupping my hipbone, the other at the dip in my back. "The complications are probably my parents' fault. And as for the confidence, it's all show," I said, "or else you're mistaking unembarrassed."

What I meant was: there have been many recent developments in my life, of which you are only one. Which is to say that I am still not sure if I am like this. But at least I am complicated in a straightforward manner. Meaning that I talk a lot and I always believe what I'm saying and I always eventually say everything I'm thinking and I think too much and I am trying to decide not to think right now. No, that's not it either. "I'm not always like this."

"Well, I like the exception."

Sometimes that night I was trying to think, because it remains true that you are much too old and much too tall and this is entirely the wrong time and all of that matters very much. It is true I have been in love with someone who is not you. I have loved many people, as have you. One of these loves was in the living room of my second floor apartment knitting a scarf and waiting for me to come home, though he is recently no longer my boyfriend. And then there is that other love, yours, who will call you in the morning and ask you what you did last night.

Which I did not say because you looked at me and your eyes were a different blue then. Then you closed your eyes and I knew that you knew all of that anyway. You knew to move your tongue lightly over my top lip and into my mouth and that I was looking over your head at a photograph of a woman with red hair playing the violin somewhere I have never been. You did not know that I used to be: a gymnast, a rock climber, a house painter, a photographer, a communist. That I was once stranded on the side of the Massachusetts Turnpike for hours in a storm in a broken car until I turned the key and the engine started and I just didn't question it for the rest of the ride home. That once I took a lot of drugs and forgot how to speak. That the things that I have wanted include: a shift in the whole social paradigm, to actually faint someday, and all of the usual things: health and happiness, success and someone who has memorized the exact way my vertebrae feel under the touch of five fingers.

I closed my eyes and negotiated my finger between my tongue and yours for a moment. You stopped still and laid your hand on my shoulder. You did not know if you wanted to go on.

I said: "Well, as long as you like the exception, then I don't see the conflict," referring to your last comment.

Of course I meant that the conflict is very clear, and that it has something to do with knitting and men and women and the ways in which people come to know each other. The space between wanting and wanting while lying on top of you like that; the concave of your collarbone.

I stroked the back of your neck with the tips of my fingers and did not say that I thought then that the best I could hope for might be a controlled fall into acute longing for you. Despite all precautions I may find myself at the last moment tumbling, trembling. This made me silent. I waited for you to speak.

Things I have wanted to be when I grow up

1. When I was little I told my mother I wanted to be an architect. I spent all day drawing complicated pictures in pencil. They all represented new and better playgrounds. Playgrounds, I thought, were the wave of the future since everyone always said that children were the precious future. I thought our bright new beginning deserved not to be bored. It turned out, though, that you have to have some capacity for math in order to be an architect. When I learned that, I retired my pencil and settled for fearing for the next generation.

2. So a teacher, I decided. I pictured showing a roomful of youngsters how to read. I would give spelling words that really mattered to school kids: licentious, misanthropic, fuck you, ennui. Frightening. Then, in junior high school I had a reading teacher who showed the same film strip every day, and while it played he would take off his wooden leg and lean it up against his desk. And my history

teacher called me the Anti-Christ in front of the whole class because I said that I didn't think that we really had won the Vietnam Conflict. I realized these were the kind of people I would be working with. I also realized that when I burst into tears in history class, none of the other kids had come to my defense.

3. In high school I decided that I wanted to be a boxer. Because I wanted to commit some violence, and I wanted to do it without hatred, fear, or anger.

4. Which is also why I became an anarchist, sort of. But it turns out that I couldn't pay my rent by stomping capitalism, eradicating imperialism, and smashing the state. And making bail costs more than I thought.

5. So after I dispensed with college, I decided to be a communist. I thought of this as an adult career choice, because surely the communists would put me to work and take care of all those things like housing and food; that's what communists do. I sat in their red rooms and smoked their terrible cigarettes and we all complained about the wage system together. They told me to join a union. But then they told me that I already had to have a job to join a union. Which was really my whole problem.

6. I applied to law school after that. I could see myself standing up and yelling, I object! in defense of my clients, all of whom were class heroes. The problem was, I look terrible in suits, and lots of those guys have killed people.

7. Looking back, it occurs to me that it has always been my dream to be an astronaut. But it turns out that you have to know how to multiply and divide, and I smoke too much. Also, I'm considered a security risk because I have been arrested and I have a certain kind of hopefulness that some people call a problem with authority. And anyway, in order to be an astronaut you have to have grown to over five feet three inches. Though I won't be thirty for a while yet, and I am sure that I won't start shrinking for many years and I should know because I am temporarily a medical receptionist, I'm pretty sure I can't hope for more than five two.

What We Would Find Out

LATER THAT DAY WE WOULD find out that: Jason's hands are a little sticky, like a child's might be. But he is moving them insistently, like a man, up her sides, under her shirt, and around her back to where her bra clasps.

This is what Lucindy knows: She knows that she would scream, or maybe not scream, but she knows she would say: stop, stop, if her voice weren't caught somewhere between her groin and her stomach, somewhere maybe in her large intestines. Her head feels heavy and she is trying to push him off of her but he too is heavy with drink and adolescence and purpose. Her friends are downstairs, gathered on the couch or lying on the floor drinking gin and Kool-Aid or cheap beer, basking in the parentless afternoon, and they would hear her if she could scream. Lucindy focuses on the window. It is still light outside, though it won't be for long, because it is winter. His fingers are digging into her flesh. She is looking at the bare branches of a tree outside and thinking that this cannot be happening at three-thirty in the afternoon, when he gets her pants off. She tries again to stop him with a word or a gesture, but all that escapes her is a groan. And Jason's hand is tugging down the right side of her underwear. She feels damp and hot, like she has a fever. Her shoes are still on and her feet, hanging off the end of the bed, feel enormous. Her underwear is down around her ankles now, restraining her from opening her legs very wide. Lucindy tries to roll off the side of the bed, but Jason stops her, and pins her with his knees, and shoves his hand between her legs.

Stop.

Twenty-one years ago Jason Jacob's mother fell in love with a man who is clinically retarded. Everyone knew this. Both of their children were born with normal intelligence. When Jason was four years old, he stepped on a nail in their backyard. His mother was speeding to the hospital with Jason in the front seat of the car when she hit a patch of black ice. The car rolled four times. Presumably, Jason watched her die while they were trapped inside the car. Everyone had known for as long as we could remember that: he was alive and she was not when the ambulance got there.

We did not yet know that: In four months Jason would get into a fight in the parking lot behind the school. Rusty Green would punch Jason once, in the face, so hard he would have a seizure. I am the one who will call the ambulance.

What I Really Meant Was That I Loved You

I SAID THESE THINGS TO YOU, I said: I think only people who have never been arrested have sex with handcuffs on (but if you remember, that was when we were watching that movie and it was funny because of the other time, at the anti-war protest, when we got arrested together), and afterwards I said I didn't want to tell you what my position on Palestine is (as it turned out, of course, I had one too many drinks and I did talk about Palestine, and unexpectedly we agreed on a two state solution), once, in the middle of the night, I asked, are you going to die? (apropos of universal health care, you had told me you have a heart condition and I wanted to know if it was a metaphor), and later I also said to you: so it's war now, is it? (but that was only because *The Herald* ran that headline, IT'S WAR!, many months after the war had been declared and a couple months after the president said it was over), and I said that the only way to subvert the militant patriarchal hierarchy was to fundamentally change the structure and nature of organized society by allowing anyone on the bottom to be on the top (it was probably the wrong time), but after all that I asked you if, really, you thought that, you know, considering, the ends could ever justify the means, like those suicide bombers exploding their desperate rapture all over public markets; and the thing is, you never answer me about the end.

Dear Mr. President

Dear Mr. President,

Right after you run your fingers, one at a time, through the hair directly above my ear, you start talking about Social Security, but I cannot forget the fact that you are 35 years older than me. Even in my dream I know that you are much more likely to benefit from all of the policies that you advocate than I am. Viagra, though wonderful for our relationship, will not mask the fact that I started working when I was fourteen and still have no faith that I will retire before I die or the planet implodes.

I know that you wouldn't have gone gray if you didn't have such enormous daily responsibility. And yes, your power was what attracted me to you in the first place. But here's why I have to break it off: after September 11th, I heard a lot of people your age compare the destruction to Pearl Harbor, to the explosion of American barracks in Africa, to what our bombers did in Yugoslavia, to Vietnam. I said: I am 21 years old. This does not remind me of anything. My hair turned gray anyway.

In my sex fantasy, while you and I are naked, my mouth covering your left nipple, I ask you for the last time: what is the opposite of death and destruction? Because I'm not sure, but I don't think that it is sex with you. Or anything with you. Not tonight. Not in my dream.

Sincerely,
Amy

62 Jokes About Elizabeth Taylor

WHEN SHE VISITED HIM THAT TUESDAY, the first thing he said to her was that he knew sixty-two jokes about Elizabeth Taylor. She thought maybe he was confused by the pain medication. Or maybe, she thought, he had really learned sixty-two jokes from his roommate, an old man asleep now with the television still tuned to Dr. Phil, but normally and ridiculously gregarious. And then she was afraid that they would be sad jokes, or would seem so here. She settled the flowers she had brought in a vase on his bedside table, to give herself a moment to think, or not to think. Then it occurred to her that this might be the joke, that it was supposed to be uproariously funny to tell people that you knew sixty-two jokes about Elizabeth Taylor and then watch their expression. She laughed so hard she cried.

Perestroika

I TOLD MY GIRLFRIEND she was being ridiculous. "It's the end of the eighties," I said, and I tossed her her hairspray to prove it. "It's the end of an era. Everything is about to change." As she teased up her bangs, I slipped my arm around her from behind, and moved my hand up under her shirt, over her bra, thinking of my high school girlfriend in the backseat of my car. I started tugging down her skirt and said, "Hey, even the Berlin Wall has come down." My girlfriend glared at me in the mirror and side-stepped out from under my hand. "You're a pig," she said, "and you're getting a zit on your forehead." My girlfriend, who wouldn't officially leave me until reunification was complete, had decided that we would not have a personal perestroika that night. I tell her we should stay home and make love because it is New Year's and because we need to mark this new decade, and because this should be our year, and because everything is about to change. She just says she's heard it all before, pulls on her leggings, and heads out to the party her best friend's room- mate is throwing in a downtown hotel room. I trail along in her wake and spend the rest of the night drinking too much and doing some blow and impersonating Slash. We will hold on for one more year, until bits of that wall are for sale and it felt like nothing would ever be the same again.

The Exact Reason There Has Been a Car in Our Front Yard for Four Years

A FORD F-150 HAS PULLED UP onto our front lawn. A kid I went to high school with is climbing out of the truck. His name is Joe, I think. Unless that was the name of his buddy and his name is Dwayne. We had math together, but he had a talent for auto body. He's circling the car that has been in our front yard for four years and for the last three has had a very faded orange sign stuck under the wipers that says FOR SALE. He is peering in through the windows and running his hands over the door handles with the weeds and a few refugee geraniums from my mother's old garden growing entwined around them. He has crouched down to check out the undercarriage.

It was my younger sister's and it is a VW Fox and it was the alternator that went that day. Although the whole thing happened a long time ago and my sister says she can't actually remember if the alternator or the starter was the problem. The alternator died one mile away from the gas station where I worked that summer and six miles away from the house. When my sister tells this story she emphasizes she walked the whole mile and there are no sidewalks on that road, but I'm pretty sure she hitchhiked. When she got there she called our dad and told him she had to have the car towed to Smitty's, which was the name of the gas station I was working at. Really what she meant was she needed some money for the tow and the repair and also a ride home. But my dad told her she couldn't bring it to Smitty's because he owed Smitty money and anyway he could fix a goddamn starter himself. I looked at the books sometimes when I got bored and it is true my father owed Smitty over two hundred dollars. I know my father would like me to point out now that Smitty was skimming off my paychecks and eventually someone turned him in to the EPA for pouring anti-freeze and used motor oil down storm drains. On the phone, though, dad just told her to go back and wait by the car and he would take care of it. My sister and I always stop at this fact, when we are telling the story, to note that my father knows nothing about cars. He won't admit this in his version, of course. And I place particular stress on the idea that my sister knew, even then, that our father knows nothing about cars, but she never could stand up to him the way I do. My mother says of course he tried to do something he was unprepared and unqualified to do, which is what he always does and never learns, because learning requires admitting you can be wrong, and all this is the reason she is living with her friend Bethany these days. But on that distant day my sister went back to her car and waited for our father with the hazards on. My father drove up in the one-ton he used to haul cement for his business. It is true I wasn't there. I was at Smitty's making five dollars an hour, but it is undeniable that my father drove up and idled next to my sister's VW Fox. My father and my sister were the only ones there and they insist he was driving his Chevy Celebrity. And I guess he must have been, because really nothing that happened would have worked if he had been in the one-ton. But I like to picture him in the truck anyway because that is how I want to think of my father, before the business went under, and up high in his truck which was the exact color of the sky before it rains. My mother would like me to remember she paid for half of that truck and never recouped the loss because, she reminds me, she never formally divorced my father, which is for my sake and the sake of my sister. So he was there, in the Celebrity, and my sister was in the Fox and staring at him, when he realized he didn't have any tow straps. My father wants me to believe he owns tow straps, but they were in the one-ton. My sister knows for a fact he never owned tow straps, or at least in her whole life she has never seen them. If my father were recounting that afternoon he would give here many technical details having to do with acceleration and angles and power steering; after a couple drinks he might even use the word inertia, which is a word he heard someone on PBS talking about. My sister mostly talks about whiplash. But I think the essential detail is that when he got the Celebrity behind her car and started accelerating, the first thing that happened was all the taillights broke at once and scattered red plastic over the road. Dad maintains the main thing is he did get her home. Mom always wants me to tell everyone the car is still in the front yard, whereas she is currently residing three towns to the south, which is better than the north because it is closer to the city where they have things like nice restaurants and public transportation.

I know that I should go out and tell Dwayne that I am sure it was just the alternator. I should mention that it can be replaced for under two hundred dollars, which he would know already but probably appreciate hearing out loud. The car was used when we got it, but nevertheless it still to this day has only eighty-thousand miles on the odometer. And of course Dwayne will be thinking that it could be used for parts. It occurs to me that he could make much better use of what we have than my family ever could.

Elvis on the Rooftop

MARYBETH TOOK ME OUT on the roof that night. The moon was fat and it shone on us. It was easy to think that it shone only on us, as if to share in our secrets, as if to say: I know. As Marybeth reached in a pocket for her lighter, one strap of her bra slipped down from underneath the cover of her white tank top. It was all over for me at that moment, but I didn't know that then. When she lit my cigarette she told me she was Elvis, though yesterday it had been Jesus. This night, the night she was Elvis, was before I understood that it is all the same. It was twenty-seven minutes before we would make love for the first time. Fourteen years before I would be married to another woman, seventeen years before my divorce, and a week before Marybeth would disappear for the first time. I would quit smoking two years and three months after that night. I would graduate from college and learn to forget some things. But I didn't know that then. The moon turned to stare. All is understood when you're Elvis on the rooftop.

How to Burn a House

I USED TO LIVE WITH YOU near two convenience stores and a large plastic cow. The guidebooks would have said The Beautiful Allegheny River. But what I remember is this. The town was on fire that year. It started with the Tierneys' barn; it was lightning, but that must have been what gave everyone the idea. Three dead cars went up after that, two smoldering down to twisted hulls in lawns on side streets, the third was merely singed by the time some zealous volunteer firemen from the high school screeched up. Some farmers burned their crops as prayer or penance, but possibly they do this every year. The trailer on the widowed Mrs. Boulier's property burned from the inside out, wooden cabinets and old linoleum curling the kitchen into nothing around the more durable corrugated aluminum. She got a small amount of insurance money for that, though everyone knew she hadn't touched it since she built her split-level then took the wheels off. Of course some smaller stuff, chimneys and appliances, the usual grease spatters like tiny firework bursts. When the kids tried to do that cow the accelerant burned so quickly the plastic spots and one of the big, sad, plastic eyes were the only things really melted. Some people said it gave her a wise look. We were, at the time, unclear about the difference between the meteor shower in August and stars dying. We thought that, like a light bulb when the filament is giving up, stars would burn brightest at the end. But it was the river behind the blanket factory that burned most brilliantly against the gray sky that fall, too late in the day for the foliage to compete and not yet dark. It must have been the dye in the runoff, in the wastewater. Flames high and hot and clear, all the colors of dreams.

(for Scott Thomson)

About the Author

Amy L. Clark is an assistant professor of college composition at Pine Manor College. She has had fiction published in several literary journals, including *Juked, Quick Fiction,* and *Fringe,* and her work appears in the anthology *Brevity & Echo.* She has always secretly wanted to be an astronaut.

SIXTEEN MILES
OUTSIDE OF PHOENIX

Elizabeth Ellen

||||

Acknowledgments

"Ground Rules" *Elimae*

"Big Gulp" *Elimae*

"Blood" *Elimae*

"How the Homeless Funambulist and Lonely Somnambulist Met and Shared a Melon" *Pindeldyboz*

"Eastern Standard" *The Guardian*

"Before You She Was a Pit Bull" *Monkeybicycle*

"Sixteen Miles Outside of Phoenix" *Elimae*

"Panama City by Daylight" *Elimae*

"8 x 10" *Smokelong Quarterly*

"What Was Meant" *Storyglossia*

"Conjoined" *Eyeshot*

"Lemons" *Elimae*

"Solving the Problem of Monogamy, Part I" *Quick Fiction*

"Let Me Tell You Something" *Elimae*

"Rough" *Elimae*

"The Truth and What It Did to Me" *Surgery of Modern Warfare*

"That Which Is Revealed in the Absence of Light" *Hobart*

"Three Seconds of Hope" *Opium*

"The Poet's Head Is in My Lap" *Bound Off*

Table of Contents

Ground Rules

LET'S SET SOME GROUND RULES, he says. As though we are kids on a playground. As though I am capable of not breaking any rule he sets before me. As though he just met me yesterday and hasn't yet figured this out.

Rule number one, he says: You can't write about this.

Right, I say. Of course. I won't.

Big Gulp

WE WERE DRINKING BEER out of shot glasses on my kitchen floor. You were wearing your winter coat. You said you could only stay a minute.

Another, you said. Another.

The faster I poured, the faster you bottomed up.

Whoa there. Easy, partner, I said.

But you didn't let up. You were really throwing them back.

At some point it occurred to me it would be easier to hand you the can, but when I extended my arm you waved it away.

There's something to it, you said.

To what?

To the theory that it hits you harder this way, you said, grabbing my wrist and downturning it. In smaller sips.

I've never heard that theory, I said. But it would explain a lot.

An hour later you were still here, the cans lined like conquered countries on the floor between us. You were visibly sweating. You still refused to remove your coat.

I can't stay, you said. I'm going to leave soon.

My left leg was already bridging the gap. I shifted all my weight onto it, elongating my right. Somewhere down below was you. All I had to do was lower.

Whoa there, you said. Easy does it.

My right thigh was in your hand. I hovered, waiting for your release.

Blood

WE ARE SPREAD OUT ON HER FLOOR, spread out on our backs staring up at the canopy of her bed, our makeshift sky. Our bodies open and close to one another, turn away from and toward. Amidst the cockroaches and palms. Here. In her/my/our father's house. We are spread out on our backs when she says it. Spread far enough that I have to stretch to touch my fingertips to hers; far enough that her voice feels distant and fuzzy as though reaching across a telephone wire rather than spanning the scope of the room. Spread out when she tells me how yesterday she overheard her mother telling the neighbor lady that where I come from, where I live, we have dirt for floors. She says it real plain, like she's telling me her mama made blueberry muffins again for dinner, but I don't take it that way. I push myself up onto my knees and reach out for her. I reach for her and wrap my hands around her neck. I hold her like that. I look into her face, searching it for some piece of myself that I don't find. I tell her, there's a difference between wood and dirt. I call her stupid and as I do so, feel my hands cling tighter to her flesh. I hold her like that until her face turns from red to white and somewhere in the very corners of her eyes and on the flat plains of her cheeks I find some little part of myself. And I let go.

How the Homeless Funambulist and Lonely Somnambulist Met and Shared a Melon

IT WAS THE HOMELESS FUNAMBULIST who found me in that cold, snowless January, the immense ugliness of the rotted grass visible when it should have been hidden. For nearly two years I had been going about my life a virtual somnambulist (noctambulist, if you prefer). I was, if you will recall, still cohabitating with the haptophobic strongman, rendered weak by his unconquerable fears. He and I passed through the various rooms of the house, careful not to bump elbows, no longer colliding at random. We had one of those implicit agreements not to remind the other of our existence within the confines of our dwelling. And yet, neither of us had taken the necessary steps to vacate. I fell deeper into my waking sleep, into my dreams—the only place in which I was felt, seen, heard.

It was during these same two years, he would confide in me later, that the funambulist became homeless. He was the youngest member of a family of tightrope walkers known the world over. Tragedy struck one day in June, over Niagara Falls. There was, it seems, an unaccounted wind that day. It was most unfortunate for all concerned that it blew its greatest breath just as the family was halfway across. One toppled, and the rest followed. All except the youngest, my funambulist, who had been sidelined with a broken toe, shattered the previous day by an unruly pachyderm. That day he took to walking the streets rather than the wires.

Several months later he found himself walking my street, though it was just another piece of pavement to him, with houses that were not his, families inside to which he did not belong. I was out walking as well, eyes open, not seeing, caught somewhere in between my dreams. Our paths crossed, our elbows brushed, our eyes locked.

"You look like home," he said simply, eyes still balanced on mine.

"And you resemble my dreams," I replied, unflinching.

He accompanied me to the store, and helped me pick a cantaloupe, eyeballing them for size, feeling them with his careful hands, inhaling them, contemplating their potential sweetness. At last we agreed upon the one. Pooling together the nickels and dimes from our pockets we paid for our melon, and headed back. As I entered the house that I once considered my home, he waited on the street that still felt like his. In a rush I threw open drawers, grabbing two spoons, a knife and the sodium chloride. Our tools gathered, we walked on to the park.

He cut straight and down the middle. We scooped out the seeds, tossing them to the ground, wondering if one day a garden of cantaloupe might spring up in that very spot.

By now the snow had begun to fall, dusting our lashes, our hair, falling into our melon. Then came the fatter flakes—the unavoidable, the ones that cannot be ignored. And I closed my eyes and I awoke, and he stumbled to me and steadied, and we caught the flakes on our tongues, our mouths open, frenzied now with the coolness of the snow and the sweetness of the melon.

Eastern Standard

THE PHONE RANG AND SHE SPRANG from the bed to answer it. She knew it would be him. They lived on opposite coasts and there existed between them several time zones. Still, he liked to wake her up to tell her goodnight. And, on the nights he forgot, she did not sleep well, but awoke in the morning with a peculiar feeling of restlessness.

Before You She Was
a Pit Bull

ON THE NIGHTS SHE IS TOO TIRED to return to you she comes to me. She slinks across town after dark and stands on my porch waiting to be let in. She raps on my door with her bloodied knuckles and pushes the uncombed locks of hair from her face as I watch from my darkened hall, unready to let her in.

She never looks so beautiful

As this: as when she is made to wait.

Not that you would know this.

She tells me about you.

She tells me how you can't go five seconds without hurling yourself at her, so eager are you to see your blood and spit and tears on her hands.

She tells me how you wait for her in your drive.

How you run into the headlights like a frightened fawn.

How before she has even stepped from the car you are between her knees, a palm on each hip, anchoring yourself to her.

She tells me what you're doing to her.

How it's killing her, this taking care of you.

She waits for me and I watch her mouth redden and soften, reminding me of the pomegranate arils I placed one at a time on her tongue that first night she was not with you. I unlock the door and open it to her, fighting the urge to bloody her lips with my teeth. Unlike you I am a master of restraint. Unlike you I can withhold my longings. I stand aside and let her take the stairs before me. I watch as she glides up them, her head cast downward, her waist more emaciated than I remembered it, her body casting canine shadows on my wall: a greyhound or a whippet, a timid creature with its tail between its legs. This is what you have made of her. Alongside you she has become weakened and I miss her strengths.

As she nears the top I think that I might have to carry her the last few steps but she drags herself to the landing and I meet her there. I guide her to the bath and sit next to her on the painted tiles, watching the steam rise from the tap and fill the room, easing our breaths and clouding our reflections. I help her disrobe and take her elbow as she steps carefully over the side and into the water. I leave my clothing on the floor beside hers and fold myself in behind her, reaching around with all four limbs, warming her body with my own.

I dampen a washcloth and gently remove the taste of you from her skin. Your fingerprints are everywhere and I am careful to wash away each one. I rake her matted hair with my fingers and feel it fall against my chest, blanketing my indecencies. I close my eyes and wish for once to be like you. I wish not to be a woman as I am but to be a man as you are. I wish for the simplicity of conveying to her my desires with the hardening of myself beneath her. How easy it could be, being you, voicing my wants and needs with only my flesh. What an injustice it is then that you waste what you have been given, that you deny her that which would satiate her; that you allow your fears of completion to come between you.

She tells me everything.

I light us a cigarette and place it between her lips where I want to be and listen to the laundry list of your requests.

She tells me how in the beginning they excited her.

How she looked forward to tightening the ropes and loosening your bowels.

How she sat in bed at night imagining new ways to unleash your tears.

She wanted to be creative. She wanted there to be an element of surprise when she marred your skin or stole your breaths.

She didn't want to be just another of your devotees going through the motions, feigning an interest in your degradations.

But now it is just another shit job, she says.

Just another eight hours to get through.

She tells me there's nothing in it for her anymore.

How your promises of reciprocation have all but been forgotten in your near constant quest for humiliation.

She tells me that above all she has grown bored with you.

There's no imagination, no ingenuity or cleverness, in your requests anymore.

Your narcissism no longer feels romantic.

She leans back into me, elongating her neck, offering up to me her mouth.

I drop the cigarette into the water and watch it float beneath her fingers.

Her body is unfamiliar to me and my first instinct is one of penetration, which leaves me feeling crippled in my body, castrated by my creator.

In time, however, our movements slow and become synchronized, our bodies mirrored images of themselves. And I let go my envy of you, of what I am not.

The nights she comes to me are beginning to outnumber those she goes to you.

Wait for her in your drive as I lie beside her counting her pretty breaths.

Continue your watch.

Pace up and down, back and forth, like a tiger in a cage, like it's your freedom you want.

Sixteen Miles Outside of Phoenix

AND IF YOU WANT TO TALK PRIDE, baby boy, I'd just as soon punch you in the gut. If you'd planned on bringing me to my knees with a word like cadence you should probably quit the business right now.

Panama City by Daylight

MY DAUGHTER WAS IN THE TUB. This was Tuesday: bath day. I had a far off look on my face. My body was in the bathroom, kneeled, before her. My mind was somewhere else: Memphis, maybe, or Moscow. "You're falling out of love with him, aren't you?" she asked. And by him she of course meant you. "No," I said. "There are ebbs and flows in relationships. This is a time of ebb. That's all." "You're not a very good girlfriend," she said, before submerging herself under water. She was practicing holding her breath. I was supposed to be counting the seconds.

You asked me the same question last week. You said, "You seem distant." Which was your version of "You don't love me as much anymore, do you?"

I was in Hattiesburg then but I didn't admit so.

"No," I said. "I'm right here."

I offered you a weak smile and dove into the pool. I floated to the bottom and made a tidy home on the floor. I turned on my side like I do in bed with you. I closed my eyes, slowed my breathing. I can stay down here a long time, I thought. I was halfway to Tallahassee already; I planned on making Panama City by daylight.

8 x 10

IN AN UNFAMILIAR ROOM YOU DISROBE, removing only bra/no panties, as previously discussed, as heretofore agreed to. An hour ago you sent your husband into the corner 7-11 for diapers and he returned with a porcelain rabbit and pack of chewing gum. His character has recently come into question. His entire act is up for review. You feed his child with a breast he begrudgingly shares while on the other side of the wall he entertains an unsuspecting audience with his one-man show. "I'm going to shoot that kid," he says, making a gun of his thumb and forefinger and pointing it at the right temple of the man in the mirror. "I used to snort cocaine off a model's ass. Those days are over," he continues, arms in the air, pausing for dramatic effect.

In the 8x10 broom closet where they store him he will refuse to open his mouth. No more soliloquies, the doctor will tell you with a smile and a handshake, as though bad theatre were ample enough reason for the removal of a tongue. Left alone with your husband you stare at him through the glass above the door and he stares back at you, his eyes static, his mouth a single straight line: _____. You study him, remembering how it feels to stand before the ocelot at the zoo: like unmitigated self-pity, like you could move the bars with your eyes if only he'd lift a paw to help.

Watch now the baby grow fat. Watch her gorge herself on your milk, forgetting what it means to share. Read to her from her book of ABCs. "O" is for ocelot, you say, remembering that the average life span of an ocelot is 10-13 years in the wild, 20 in captivity.

What Was Meant

SHE DIDN'T MEAN WHAT SHE SAID. I'm fairly certain of that. Or, if she did mean what she said, she probably didn't mean for what she said to come out the way that she said it. Perhaps she didn't mean for it to come out at all. I remember she turned her head slightly to the left afterward (I was on her right), a gesture I interpreted at the time as regret, though it is possible, in hindsight, that she turned her head to the left to clear her view (she has very long hair, this woman) and the thought of regret never even entered her mind. I want to give her the benefit of the doubt. I have not known her long. She is not one of my oldest friends. She is not, technically, my friend at all. She is the wife of a friend. This is the fact I find most irritating. I am often irritated when forced to make small talk with women who are married to friends of mine. I do not like small talk and am not good at making it. I was already annoyed at being left alone with her. This was before she made the remark in question. Perhaps if I had not been so annoyed I would not have been listening quite as carefully to what she was saying and would not now be hearing her words over and over again in my head as though they were an oral grocery list or set of daily affirmations. I don't want to think that she meant what she said. What she said was very unkind. If she meant the unkind thing that she said it stands to reason she is an unkind person and if she is an unkind person what sort of person then is my friend, her husband? I have always believed my friend to be a kind man. Perhaps he too is unkind but is better at disguising his unkindness. I cannot remember a time when my friend acted in an unkind manner or made an unkind remark but maybe this is because I am never annoyed at being left alone with him and therefore pay little attention to the things he does and says. It is possible he has made many unkind comments in my presence over the years. He has very unusual eyes, my friend, the color of molasses, and I often find myself staring into them as though held in place by a visual stickiness. His wife's eyes are not unique. They are blue or green or some combination of the two. They are a color you would expect.

The Pen Is Mightier Than the Sword

IT REQUIRES AN ACT OF GREAT self-discipline: not sawing my mother in half. It would be such an easy trick. A magician's sleight of hand. Drawing a bubble over her head and filling in the words.

Conjoined

THE OPERATION WAS LAST WEEK. It took a team of four doctors ten hours to dislocate him from my side. We'd been joined at the hip for too many years to count and he wasn't going anywhere without a fight. But the surgeons were highly trained and skilled; his rudimentary application was no match for their nimble fingers. When all was said and done, the doctors stood over our newly detached bodies, shaking hands and slapping backs, admiring their handiwork. We were proclaimed a success.

We lay there a while longer, unable yet to stand, each on our own feet. We had risen and descended simultaneously for so long as one entity, it felt entirely foreign and more than a little awkward, to attempt such basic, unsynchronized movement independent of one another. The first steps are always the hardest.

But this is what I wanted, I reminded myself. This is what I had argued and fought for, dreamt about and anticipated, for the latter half of our union. It was just going to take some getting used to. It was perfectly within reason to feel overwhelmed and apprehensive immediately following separation. I recalled having once read about blinded people who were sighted through surgery. Suicidal feelings were not uncommon in the days and weeks thereafter. The visual world, which they had lived in the shadows of for so long, was too much for them. It was the darkness that they knew, in which they felt safe and secure.

I looked over at Ping. He seemed so small and vulnerable lying there alone with his limbs and organs all to himself. I realized I had no knowledge of how he appeared from a distance greater than six inches. To me, from my vantage point aside his hip, he had always seemed strong and virile. Now he appeared as fragile as a newborn fawn. I wondered how his legs would ever hold him.

I was filled briefly with misgivings and self-doubt, questioning my desire for autonomy. I turned away from his pleading eyes and choked back all feelings of regret. There was no time for them. Now was the time for independence and self-discovery, for forging ahead as one, lighted now by the removal of his body, which had become like an unwelcome tumor weighing me down, encumbering my movement and freedom.

I left him without so much as a goodbye. It was too soon to speak. I feared his magnetic pull. I did not trust my own instincts. For the first time in years I entered the car on the driver's side. Just sitting behind the wheel, the key yet in my quavering hand, was a great empowerment. I drove away from that hospital without any predetermined destination in mind.

I drove and was intoxicated by the motion, by the perpetual push forward. But the intoxication soon waned as I realized I was dependent yet upon a force outside myself. What I really wanted, what I sought above all else, was to experience my body's own power and capabilities, without aid of another. At the next light I turned and parked the car. I got out and began walking on the sidewalk, propelled now solely by my own legs, my own muscles and blood and determination. The singularity of my stride was both dizzying and unnerving. Tears welled and fell from my eyes but I was unable to determine the reason for their existence; I was unable to distinguish joy from sorrow. My emotions were an entanglement of every feeling I had ever experienced.

At this point, overcome by vertigo and light-headedness, I found an uninhabited bench and sat perfectly still in the shadow of a single, lone oak. The oak was at once majestic and pitiful, standing tall in all of its sorrowful glory. I yearned to wrap my arms about its great trunk, to feel something other than my own skin against me. I dreamed of making myself an appendage to its side, an outgrowth of its sturdy being.

This is when the aches began, the phantom pains. They started in my western hemisphere and spread rapidly eastward, quickly overtaking my entire system. They were sharp and unwavering, and though I did my best to ignore them, to convince myself of their nonexistence, they continued undaunted by my disbelief, impairing my breaths and confusing my thoughts. I walked on, hoping the continued movement might relieve some of my discomfort. But instead the pain became more acute, swelled and magnified, reaching now to my heart. I feared it might cease pumping in the face of so much hurt.

I retreated to the car and with every ounce of strength and clarity I could muster, drove back in the direction of the hospital. I could feel my body weakening, my joints stiffening and my organs atrophying. I looked at the clock and drove faster.

Ping was waiting for me just outside the door, leaning up against the brick wall for support. With all my remaining might I ran to him and with a level of faith I had heretofore thought only a fool could possess, knew that once united, our bodies would cease their deterioration and once more thrive. With a rush of adrenaline I jumped and impaled myself upon his body, encircling his waist with my trembling thighs, crushing his chest with the weight of my own.

I prayed it wasn't too late. I hoped the doctors had not yet left the building. There was no question reattachment was in order. This time, however, attachment of the hips would not be enough. This time I wanted to adhere myself to his very core. This time we would leave no room for scalpels, no leeway for dismantlement.

Lemons

You come home from work to find your husband on his knees, a televangelist on the screen before him, the knife you used to cut your wedding cake at his wrist. Odd, you think then lock yourself in the bathroom with a magazine and the cookie sheet you keep under the couch. Proceed as normal, your thoughts caution as you strike a match against your heel. Remember the one about the guy who ate so much acid he thought he was an orange? When you said I do you never bargained you'd end up eating citrus fruit for dinner. You should have demanded a prenup.

When life hands you lemons, spit the seeds into oncoming traffic. You read that once on the inside of a matchbox in ____, South Dakota. This was on your honeymoon, before the incident with the anesthesiologist. Your husband ran barefoot through fields of sunflowers every time you stopped to take a piss. You came to despise the color yellow. It burned a hole through the rearview mirror. You kept your gaze straight ahead.

In the morning an impatient woman will ask your husband his religion and he'll tell her to go to hell. For this he will be given a room without a view. She will fail to see the humor in his delivery. She will choose to focus on the words instead. Taken out of context, you'll say but she'll turn her back. She has a line of people whose religions are unaccounted for. You walk your husband down the hall with a mouthful of pulp. Spit.

Solving the Problem of Monogamy, Part I

IT WAS WHILE SCRAPING the last bits of residue from the bowl and watching *Helter Skelter* at three o'clock in the morning that she had the idea for the commune. She began immediately to make a list. After ten minutes she had three names. An hour later she still had only the original three, though two more had been added and crossed out. The list-making tired her. She fell asleep in her clothes atop the bed. In the morning she awoke excited to share her idea with her husband. She went into the living room to retrieve her list. Her husband was already there, watching TV and smoking the bowl. The list was on the coffee table. A name had been added in red pen. She read it carefully as one reads a death threat or ransom note. She looked at her husband, shredding the list into pieces and fitting them one at a time into her mouth. She wondered where he kept his red pen.

Let Me Tell You Something

I AM NOT WELL.

Something feels off kilter. The liquid in my ears, maybe.

Or something else entirely.

Walking down the hallway toward you I stumble twice. I have to steady myself on the wall. I have to stop and think before retying my shoe.

When you feel you would be willing to drink the bath water of the person seated across from you, that's when you know you are screwed.

"I think I am no longer capable of falling in love," you say and I laugh as though this is the funniest thing you have ever told me.

Rough

THE NEW PUPPY PISSES on the floor and you make no move to clean it. You sit on the tile six inches away and stare blankly as he runs back and forth through his own mess. The old you would have had seven kinds of bleach out by now. The old you would be on her hands and knees scrubbing until every trace of uncleanliness was removed from the ground.

Your hands are already growing softer. The cracks at the sides of your fingers are almost healed. You no longer have to wrap them in bandages at night.

"Why are your hands so rough?" you remember him asking. This was the night he had to hold you by the wrists in order to avoid coming into contact with other parts of you.

The Truth and What It Did to Me

THE TRUTH DID NOT SET ME FREE. The truth looked at my hand extended in friendship and spat on it. The truth rammed its tongue down my throat, then chastised me for not speaking. The truth bound and gagged me, then turned me over and fucked me up the ass before calling me a whore. The truth threw me to the floor then ran to the bathroom to clean itself of me. The truth returned, drying its hands on a hand towel, then called me a bitch and tossed my pillow on the couch. The truth cried itself to sleep for the sins it had committed against fidelity. In the morning, the truth took me to breakfast, but couldn't break a hundred.

Abandoning the truth soon thereafter, I set out in search of a deception. It wasn't hard to find. It came in and sat down next to me at the bar down the street. I knew it right away when it began by calling me beautiful and buying me a drink. It continued, the deception, by escorting me to dinner, taking my elbow, guiding me gently, draping my chilled shoulders with its jacket as we walked through the night air.

Later, in the darkness of my room, I pulled the deception to me, running my fingers through its hair, my tongue down its neck, tasting the salt of its crocodile tears. I climbed into its lap and made myself at home. The deception told me it loved me and I chose to believe it.

All night long, I made love to the deception. All night long, I said to myself, fuck the truth and its need to be heard. Fuck the truth and its self-righteousness. Fuck the truth and its withholding of emotion. Fuck the truth and its lack of affection. Fuck the truth, fuck the truth, fuck the truth.

That Which Is Revealed
in the Absence of Light

THIS WAS THE NIGHT THE LIGHTS went out. In a wavering second the whole house fell first dark and then silent, in mimicry of the rest of the houses on the block. Breaking the unsettling quiet were the shrieks and squeals of the youngest inhabitants, those who did not fear the dark but were enlivened by the vast possibilities it held. They found me in the shadows, came rushing to my sides, arms extended, reveling in the musical reverberations of their own voices amid the silence. They grasped and tugged at my sleeves, taking me captive, dragging me into their magical lair, where bears and tigers mixed with unicorns and narwhals in a utopian kingdom in which predatory instincts gave way to peaceful civilities.

"Play with us," they, my captors, commanded. And I, unable to refuse them, began the gathering of necessary provisions.

We sat in a semicircle around our makeshift campfire upon their floor, the flickering candle offering little light and littler heat. The giant roamed the vacated rooms below us, misunderstood and neglected. With our gowns pulled tight about our crossed legs and our mouths sweetened with the squares of chocolate we stuffed neatly into them, we took turns telling the stories we saved for these darkened moments.

I went first. Mine was about two little girls—not princesses, but explorers. This pleased them. They, in turn, relayed tales of panthers and spider monkeys—jungle menageries discovered in the deepest pockets of forgotten forests.

The house grew cold about us. The chilled air brought visibility to the words emitted through our dragon breath. Seeking warmth and comfort we crossed over the gorge that separated our rooms and climbed as one into my bed. I lay in the middle, pilfering their heat, a tousled mane on each shoulder. We pulled the layering of blankets and quilts over our heads and took turns conjuring creatures in the flashlight's shadow until we could no longer breath and rose begrudgingly to the surface for air.

The youngest fell asleep first, her mouth agape in slumber, warming my arm with her baby's breath. I watched as her eyes fluttered beneath closed lids, lost to me in her dinosaur dreamland. With a mother's hungry heart I took her hand gently in mine, lifting the tips of her pink fingers to my mouth, bestowing each one with wish-filled kisses.

From the other side of the bed, from a distance both grand and insignificant, came the muffled sobs of her sister, of the one I had not myself bore. The sounds of her cries startled me. In the five years that had passed since the giant first introduced me to her toothless grin, I had seen her cry only once, after a mob of angered wasps had circled and attacked her trespassing legs. My heart opened wider to her and my arms followed suit. She turned neither toward nor away from me, but allowed herself to be held in my embrace.

It is a well-known but oft-forgotten fact that children are unable to tell lies in the dark. With adults you can never be certain. Some can, some can't. It depends upon the retained permeability of their heart.

I waited for her cries to wane.

"Tell me your secrets," I said, having never before thought to ask.

"I'm afraid of never seeing you again," she whispered, her face turned toward the wall, fearing my response.

On the other side of the frosted window a For Sale sign stood stiff in the frozen ground. The giant and I had agreed to part ways. It was only a matter of time.

"Shall I tell you my secret?" I asked, dabbing her wet eyes with the back of my sleeve.

She nodded through a yawn.

"It is the same as yours," I confided. "And when two people share the same fear, it could also be said that they share the same wish. And if two people share the same wish, it's bound to come true."

On into the night we whispered, exhausting all our kept secrets and fears and wishes. We made promises that night, promises that we sealed with a needle's prick, with the blood that oozed and mixed atop both our fingers. Later, our minds at peace, our bodies limp, we closed our eyes aside one another, lulled into sleep by the steady breaths of the youngest, the fearless of our trio.

Sometime in the night I heard the heat kick on.

This was three years ago. They watch the storms more closely now. With crossed fingers and hopeful eyes they watch and wait. They wait for the lights to once again be extinguished. They wait for me to call them to me, my voice guiding them through the darkness. They wait for a lone candle to be lit, for its flickering emulations to illuminate our expectant faces, signifying the beginning of storytelling time. They wait, chocolates and graham cracker squares stacked neatly before them, lions and tigers at their sides, for me to tell them the story that begins, "Once upon a time there were two sisters, not princesses, but explorers. Into the deepest and darkest of jungles they trudged, hand in hand, unafraid."

Three Seconds of Hope

FOR ALL OF THREE SECONDS this morning your dream world and conscious world overlapped, and you were happy. For three seconds you actually believed he was moving back, that once more he would be on the same side of the Mississippi as you, and that surely you were the reason for this sudden relocation. For three seconds you were smiling with eyes yet to open.

With that fourth second the eyes popped wide, the smile headed south, and with these things the realization that it had all been a dream. In that fourth second he remained thousands of miles from you. In that fourth second you were once more alone.

As second number five passed you rolled back over onto your sinking stomach, pulling the covers up over your head, wanting nothing more to do with reality, hoping to fall back into the dream, back to him.

The Poet's Head
Is in My Lap

THE POET'S HEAD IS IN MY LAP, his legs entwined between mine. The Poet is wearing tennis shoes and a jean jacket and doesn't look like a poet at all. My surprise at seeing him for the first time this morning did not escape his notice. "You thought you were in the wrong room," he smiled into my ear an hour later in the pub across the street. And I shyly nodded and hid my face which was flushed both from the warmth of the bar and the directness of his questioning, in the lining of his jacket. Our speech by then had been liberated by the half pints of ale that slid too easily down our throats and swelled our otherwise empty stomachs.

The Poet bears little resemblance to the photo on the jacket of the book currently between my fingers. The man in the small black and white photograph has neatly cropped hair, large muscles, and angry eyes. The man in the photograph looks dangerous. I stare at him, imagining his heavy fists raised in the air, ugly words spewing forth from his clenched mouth. The man whose cheek is pressed firmly to my belly is not dangerous. His small body is curled and twisted around mine, offering passersby the impression of a child resting safely within the confines of his mother's body.

We, The Poet and I, are nestled in the warm grass, sharing the lawn with similarly entangled pairs of bodies on this cloudless spring afternoon. I am unaccustomed to drinking during the day and the heaviness of my head confirms this fact. I am unaccustomed also to men I have just met falling asleep stretched out overtop my abdomen, their fingers traveling upwards beneath the stiff fabric of my shirt, preferring the softness of my skin, and yet, here is The Poet, asleep beneath my gaze, warming my middle with his unlabored breaths. The sun inches tentatively across the sky. The Poet's head rises and falls. More rapidly now I turn the pages of his book, lost to the words within, rushing through them toward an end, momentarily forgetting their creator in so doing.

For twenty minutes or half an hour or long enough for the sun to pass between the branches of the tree overhead, The Poet rests, does not stir, remains peaceful in his stillness, until, eventually, perhaps sensing somewhere in his subconscious my abandonment of him, he moves, turns and tosses, emits from a place I cannot see a low moan like the call of a calf, and I turn immediately to him. I stroke his head, smooth the hair from his face, soothe him back into slumber with whispered words of affection like the lover I am not. And when his body is content and motionless once more, I turn again to the book, which speaks to me as he cannot.

His poetry is logged complaints, tales of unanswered longings and hijacked lovers.

It speaks indulgently of motherless men seeking redemption in the arms of wayward women, anchoring themselves unsuccessfully to their restless bodies and being cast unapologetically aside.

I read with one hand holding the book, the other cradling. The Poet's head. I read and am undone by his story. I read and am enamored by his needs, which are many.

I read and am overcome with the knowledge that I alone will be the assuager of his fears. I will stay with you, I tell him through pressed lips. I will stay and hold you as you wish to be held. I will clutch you to me day and night. I will not tire nor waver in my purpose.

I will place you on your back and preside over you with the strength of ten men.

I will wipe clean your memories with one well-positioned knee to the throat.

I will quell your nightmares with one hand over your nose and the other covering your mouth. I will do the things the other women would not. I will do the things of which you were too ashamed to speak.

The Poet's body grows heavy overtop me, reminding me of my weighted bladder. The sun is a constant presence on our backs, creating a pooling layer of moisture between our bodies and a pounding in my head. My legs, confined between his, have begun to ache and my eyes jump from page to page, overlooking the words they deem unimportant, racing ahead to the acknowledgments.

His poetry has made an amnesiac of me. I have forgotten, in my study of his confessional lines, my own poems, yet unpublished, sitting in a neat stack upon my desk. In my intoxication with his language I failed to remember my own linguistic call for a lover, someone who will take me on his knee, allow me to sleep folded like a small child or pet upon his lap, let me call him daddy when I am good and wash my mouth out when I am not.

We could take turns, I stupidly think. On Mondays, Wednesdays and Fridays I will address his wants, answer his questions, meet his unmet needs. Tuesdays, Thursdays and Saturdays he will reciprocate. Sundays we will rest. Sundays we will play Scrabble and Cribbage and Parcheesi. Sundays we will be the quiet couple you see at Denny's, sharing a Grand Slam, buttering our toast.

The Poet suddenly unwinds his legs, dislocates his limbs, liberates himself from my body. The Poet sits up, speaks of his desires: for coffee, a bathroom, a place to write.

We walk awkwardly down the street, two separate entities, unhinged from one another at last.

We part as friends, each wrapping an arm shyly about the other, speaking of future meetings though we know there will be none. We part dissatisfied lovers. We part with a quiet feeling of failure. I more than he. He having long ago grown accustomed to the feeling. He having made a career of it. A life.

In Your Absence
My Awareness Is Minimal

I GO TO SLEEP AND AWAKEN with equal parts disinterest. I brush my teeth and urinate and move my bowels at the times I have grown accustomed to doing each of these things. I acquire no new chores; take up no new hobbies. I meet no new people and avoid old ones. I do not bother with confessions or admissions of love or guilt or indifference. I do not trouble my lover with such inconsequential matters for you are never coming back and to do so would only force me to summon the energy I don't have to argue the things that no longer matter; to argue things the relevancy of which has long since expired.

I make love to him with an eye to the wall, watching the hands of the clock for movement. I quicken my breath in an attempt at matching the rapidity he is used to feeling against his chest. I bend my neck and expand my arms, open my legs, shut my eyes, move in a manner that will detract him from the frigid state in which you have left me, and try not to think of you.

The impossibility of this task—of thinking of anyone but you, of anything but your wickedness and deceit and transcendent beauty, of your mouth as it curls into lies, of your fingers as they trespass against another, of your deadpan stare defying me to disbelieve you—is something I am aware of every time I crawl across the floor to someone who is not you.

About the Author

Elizabeth Ellen is the author of *Before You She Was a Pit Bull* (Future Tense). Her stories have been published in a wide variety of print and online journals, magazines, and anthologies, including *Spork, Pindeldyboz, The Insomniac Reader (Manic D), The Guardian, Quick Fiction,* and *Created in Darkness by Troubled Americans: The Best of McSweeney's Humor,* and have received nominations for The Million Writers Award as well as a Notable Mention in *The Best American Nonrequired Reader* (2002). She lives in Ann Arbor and is Deputy Editor of *Hobart*.

THE SKY IS A WELL

Claudia Smith

| | | |

Acknowledgments

"Cherry" *Failbetter*

"Possum" *Juked*

"Wildfire" *Elimae*

"Slip" *The Mississippi Review* (online)

"Colts" *Elimae*

"Mermaid" *Pindeldyboz*

"Toads" *Literary Potpourri*

"Galveston" *The Mississippi Review* (online)

"Window" *Eleven Bulls*

"Harvest Moon" *Juked*

"The Sky Is a Well" *Smokelong Quarterly*

"Angel Wings" *Pindeldyboz*

"Arson" *Opium*

"Her Lips" *Smokelong Quarterly*

* "Galveston" makes reference to the following:
  "You've Never Been This Far Before," 1973, sung by Conway Twitty, lyrics
  and music by Conway Twitty. "Galveston," 1969, sung by Glen Campbell,
  words and lyrics by Jimmy Webb.

* "Wildfire" refers to the Michael Martin Murphy song "Wildfire."

Table of Contents

Cherry

DELIA REMEMBERS THERESA'S CAR, a camel colored Pacer inherited from a half brother in Florida. Theresa wasn't old enough to have a license so she only drove it on back roads. Summer before sophomore year, they would drive to the snack shack on Saturday afternoons, get Dr. Pepper floats, then drive out to an abandoned warehouse behind the old school and make out.

"I don't ever want to go home," Delia said.

"Me either," Theresa said. "But my Mom doesn't care. I do what I want."

Delia's mother knew all about people like Theresa. "Neglected," her mother said, lowering her voice to a hiss. "That's why she doesn't know any better than to sit with her legs spread-eagled."

"Her mother sends her to Catholic school," Delia said.

"That's the grandmother's doing, " her mother answered. She wanted Delia to do something constructive with her summer. Take a Prep class. Volunteer at the Y.

Nobody would ever see them. The car was swallowed up by overgrown grass. They weren't the only ones who went out there, but they picked the daytime so they had it to themselves.

Those afternoons were lazy and still, time in between time for Theresa, Delia could tell. The hours all slip into one long memory. Snapping Theresa's bra so hard she squealed. The way she smelled, like soap and laundry and all the things Delia's Mom paid the maid to do, things that never smelled so good until they were Ther's smells. They'd unroll the windows and leave the battery running, listen to Theresa's Mom's old eight tracks. Roberta Flack, Neil Diamond, Simon and Garfunkel, stuff they complained about but that sounded right.

"I want Depeche Mode," Theresa said.

"Those guys are all gay, you know," Delia told her.

Theresa had yellow hair so shiny it looked like sun on water, cut square above her chin like Louise Brooks. She wore black lace-up boots with lovely old dresses bought from the Thrift Barn. She lived with her mother in a ratty duplex. It smelled like cat piss, she told Delia.

Theresa wanted boyfriends. Delia was just for when she felt lonely. She said she was a virgin.

"You aren't really a virgin, Ther," Delia said.

Theresa jerked away, then bent over to unlace her boots. She always wore satin ribbons or lace from her grandmother's old sewing box in place of shoelaces. Delia loved her best in her crushed velvet brown dress with brown ribbons in her boots, and a felt flapper hat she only wore at night. She called it a cloche.

"It depends on your criteria," Theresa said. "I say until your cherry is popped, you're a virgin."

They'd talk. About the boys Theresa liked. About the popular kids at school who seemed to know things they would never learn. About how much Theresa wanted breasts like Delia's, big and soft but not slutty looking. Then, Theresa would decide when it was time. She'd scooch over, drop her head in Delia's lap, or grab her wrist.

"This is the last time," Delia said.

"You always say that," Theresa said.

"It's a sin," Delia said.

Theresa said what they did was like an electric shock. But it didn't count. She hadn't done it, not the way Delia had, with a boy, with blood.

Theresa laid her head in Delia's lap.

"Put the 8 track in, Delly. I want to hear 'I Am I Said.'"

Delia was still.

Theresa took her hand, played with her fingers. She bent Delia's index finger back so far it popped.

It was getting dark, too late to leave the windows opened because mosquitoes were out. Hard to remember exactly what the sounds were from, but Delia can hear them now—crickets? Cicadas? Or were they the same thing? She doesn't remember. Fireflies flickering, and all that burned grass.

Possum

AT NIGHT I LISTENED TO RAIN on the tin roof, imagining I was in a land where it rained until the sky was full of water. They left me alone mostly, so in the mornings I could go for long walks in the woods, smelling wet dirt. The mother cooked something called collards and greens, and fried eggs served so hot they hurt the roof of my mouth. We all drank kefir, made from an aunt's goats. The mother kept a parakeet, Pretty Bird, hanging in a green cage beside the vegetable baskets. He was Pretty Bird 2; number one's legs had been fried by a boy, a boy who was gone. I came to take his place. I was easy, they said. They called me Pea and sometimes the older girls rolled my hair in big pink Velcro rollers, then blew it dry until it fell thick and straight to my shoulder blades. I had good hair, the sisters told me, it was the color of Champagne Blonde #14, what their aunt bought in bulk. I kept their used eyeshadows, periwinkle blue and carnation pink, in a music box. The box had a dancing ballerina; her tutu was gone, but her golden toe shoes were painted on. They would never get lost. They had given me their own name. In my head, I said, Pea, not Priscilla. Pea, as in princess; Pea, as in sweet little pea.

What the girls smelled of was bubble gum and Aquanet, clean like disinfectant and sweet like cake. I don't have a scent, I whispered. They giggled. Pea, you say weird things.

Oh, Pea, they said. They talked about things they did, when I was there, like the time they found one hundred dollars beside the tracks, or when the man in Mr. Fresh asked the smallest one if she wanted a free pollywog from out of his backpack, and when we asked him what a pollywog was, he walked away all funny, like he was shoplifting or cussing when he shouldn't. But they didn't talk about it like I was there; they didn't notice, or it wasn't important. Once, I said I could drink five Snow Blizzards at the Mr. Fresh and I did, and they remembered. They talked about it all night, how I gulped, my big white moustache, how my eyes got big as saucers when my brain froze. Their mother tapped my foot. Where is it? she said. Where's the hole in there?

The week before I went someplace else, it rained every night. The mother came in on the fifth night, and asked me how I was. I felt sparks were coming out of my fingers. Looks like a fever, she said, and sighed. Where does it hurt? I felt pressing in my brain. Why didn't you say anything? The last thing we need is another sinus infection. Don't you have the sense? Cripes, cripes.

When she left I crawled under the bed, with the wet magazines, sniffing rain. I kept my ear to the floor, listened to distant voices. Why doesn't she say anything? She knows how to talk in a normal voice, I hear her saying words in her sleep. Their voices were so far away, I couldn't attach them anymore. Darlene, Patricia-Patty, Miranda-Mir, the mother, Nelly.

I thought about senses, and thought I could taste what I smelled, and smell what I felt. If I could lie there on the cool green floor and listen hard enough, I would sleep and seep and sleep and fall away, dead like possums or gone where insects go after a storm.

Tempo

I FELT PEOPLE'S EYES ON ME, back then. I was white, thin without trying, usually dressed in old brown velvet and the pink ballet slippers I'd found in a dumpster the day after Halloween. A boy I liked had called me a sprite, so I decided to become one.

When I met him, he wouldn't smile. He wasn't cruel, or kind. He offered me a mug of hot water. He told me he didn't believe in using names. Looking at him was looking into water's surface. I asked him if he could teach me how to forget and he said he could teach me nothing. Years later, I'd read about the cult he joined and how they all died together waiting for something, someone to come.

I sat in his room and felt the calm of not trying for someone else. I learned to drink hot water when I was hungry. His brother came to visit and told me I was one of the only people he'd speak to now. "Really?" I asked. I barely knew him. I only studied there because he said he didn't care, and he was quiet and his place was warm and the lighting was good. Sometimes, we played chess. But he always won, and I grew bored. I only played to please him.

I knew he came from money, which made me feel an odd ache for him. I felt less than and more than someone who came from money. "I'm on scholarship," I told him. I wanted him to be impressed. I watched him as if he were a beautiful landscape. He sat at a desk with a banker's lamp, and his clothes were either tan or white, always clean the way I imagined students from another era were clean. Starched, ironed, well cared for clothes that he wore over and over again. I didn't want to touch him; it would have seemed rude.

I perfumed myself with vanilla. I came into his small house late on nights when I was too tired to drive home after my night-shift and slept on the peach cushions in his window seat. I was sloppy, but he said nothing. Mornings after, I'd boil eggs. He didn't eat; he drank water instead. Once, when I tried to do the dishes, he held up his hand to stop me. I thought he looked ridiculous, just then. A poser.

He never went to class; teachers came to him. "You think they'd let you do that if you weren't rich?" I asked him. "No," he said.

It went on like that. It got to where I needed to see him at the end of each day.

"If you don't care about worldly things," I asked him, "why do you keep this place so clean and smelling so good?" He didn't answer. He wasn't talking to me, or anyone I knew, anymore. The house he lived in on campus had belonged to an uncle, a dead professor's lover. "I bet you have a maid," I said the next night. That's how our conversations were, like shreds of correspondence. They'd pick up hours, days, after they began. When he stopped speaking, I continued speaking in the same way. I thought I could read his responses in his eyes, which were large, brown, and as expressive as an animal's.

I sipped hot water and stared at him. We sat that way for a long time, until the evening had come, then gone, and lamplight filled the room.

"You beat me," I said, and stood up. My foot was numb.

"If you want to fucking give up, go fucking right ahead," I said.

"Well, I'm going to leave now. I'm going to go outside and drink and eat until I'm puking chunks. And someday when I'm rich I'll eat and eat until I'm fat as a hat and you stay here and be thin as a pin."

I felt so heavy, outside. It was raining, just enough to make the streets shiny. I stood outside his window. It was too dark, of course, but I thought about him hard until my eyes watered and I believed I could see his body, a dark figure burned inside dark, seated there in the window. He's moved, I thought. He's moved so that I can see him.

Wildfire

I'M DRIVING PAST A GRAVEYARD and there's a song on the radio that reminds me of the girl who slipped icy cubes of urine down my back when I was in the sixth grade. She used to whistle when I walked into the room and call me double D; we were both early every day, me because my mother had to drop me off in time for work, her because her mother taught there. She wasn't popular or unpopular. I wasn't unpopular, really, either. This song is about a girl running out in the night, in a snowstorm, calling her horse's name. It made this girl cry. I laughed. We were sworn enemies. She asked me why I wore braids, was I a retard? She, herself, wore her hair in golden wings. One day I found her behind the Our Lady statue, stabbing primrose stems until juice ran down her fingers. I came up behind her and kicked her in the tender hollow of her knee. We were tearing, biting, screaming. I didn't see or feel the nun who tore us apart. Alone in the principal's office, I studied my scratches, the perfect bruises her sharp teeth had left. You should be kind, Sr. Rosa told me. She told me this girl's father liked the bottle. I envisioned a man much like my father, sucking from a baby bottle's nipple, although I knew what she meant. Biting my lip I felt a rush. It could be an hour, it could be a few minutes, passing through small towns I don't plan to drive through again, the volume down all the way so her song is in my head. Soon there are no town lights. I'd forgotten about how the girl freezes to death after running through a blizzard calling out her horse's name. No wonder she loved that song, she was crazy about horses, always drawing them in the margins of her notebooks. I feel like pulling over, finding a bar, kissing someone on the lips, hard. I can see her, sweat soaked in a white blouse worn transparent. It makes me want to cry. I don't.

Slip

THERE IS A BABY AND HE IS SO SMALL, he's smaller than a needle. Smaller than the threading hole on a needle. I had him next to me, nursing, before he shrank. Now I can't find him. He's slipped through the bed boards, or fallen through a crack in the floor.

We make goo. Goo is water and cornstarch. I scrunch up my nose. Ooo, goo, I say. My son laughs. Goo! He says. Ewww. Goo! He smears the goo over his face, he stuffs it into his mouth. I put him in the bathtub. We cover his duckies in goo. Ooo, we say. Goo.

There is a slip of a baby following me. He's a ghost baby, but not really, because he never was. He was never a baby, not completely. He is maybe not even a he. He is all of the almost-babies. The lamplight outside our windows is bright. I wake. My husband is groaning, still asleep. Outside the air conditioning unit hums. I listen to the baby monitor. Our baby is stirring. He may cry a little, go back to sleep. Now he's crying. He heard me pacing.

We fall into a shallow slumber when he nurses at night. My mother told me never to nurse a baby in bed. You could lean over, suffocate. But I would never.

Lights slip in and out of cracks, and there is some giggling, some tittering. When I was a little girl, I would see the figure of a man walking in and out of the walls. I knew the man was real and I knew he couldn't be. After I bring our baby back to his crib, I look out the window. Our apartment is in a nature preserve off the highway. You can hear the cars whoosh past the forest, if you listen hard enough. If you listen hard enough, they begin to sound like rushing water.

Colts

WE READ BOOKS ABOUT COLTS, born in milky wetness, learning to walk, and then winning races. We knew what withers and Run for the Roses were about. The willow tree in her yard was our refuge, where our horses trained, and where our dolls jockeyed championship races. We tied our dolls to the weeping willows, swung them around like children on a carnival ride. I was thin; she was plump. Her parents had sent her to fat camps; my mother said her mother was the type to want a daughter in pageants. Her parents had cocktails and little wieners on cocktail bread with pale cheese. We drank the leftover liquor and fought over the glasses without melted ice. Our mothers didn't like one another, but recognized the value of girls and their secrets. Sometimes, we snuck into her father's desk and stole his letters. She never came to my house, but I told her about the loose change my father left on the dresser, how I took it to buy jewelry from the mall. Her father kept a stash in the liquor cabinet. My father was a cop. Her father was a lawyer. Our mothers both wore dark glasses, hiding their marks behind scarves and migraines. We compared their bruises as if they were badges. We tied our dolls to the trees by their necks. We hanged the cowardly women.

Mermaid

MY SISTER KILLED HERSELF the week I turned eight. Three days before my birthday. We didn't celebrate. That afternoon, I walked along the beach in my bare feet and filled my pockets with shells. I found some seahorses, but threw them away because they stank. I found a sand dollar. They were rare. My sister always found them but I never had. She'd told me once that if you crumbled them the right way, they would divide into pieces that looked like doves.

I crushed the sand dollar. The day was cold so I kept my hands inside my pockets, and just felt the broken pieces. I thought about the scar on my index finger, where she'd smashed a cracked shot glass over my knuckle. I pulled out the finger and kissed the white lines across my knuckles. She had a temper.

Her room was painted aqua blue. Not the color of our ocean, the color of postcard oceans we had never seen. Our ocean was gray, and on cold days, almost as black as oil. Only five days before my birthday, she'd walked along the water with me and told me that once, she'd seen a mermaid behind some driftwood, through the corner of her eyes. She had only caught a glimmer, and had been afraid to look again. She knew the mermaid would either be beautiful or terrible to look upon. She liked telling me stories, she liked pretending Santa was real and she wanted me to stay a little kid. I told her I believed her. Then she asked me if I ever wondered what it felt like, to live someplace where there was no light, at the bottom of the sea.

Toads

Netti, what is a dingleberry, exactly? My little sister asked
me. I didn't know, but I wasn't going to tell her that. Dingle
sounded like jingle.

Some kind of bell-shaped berry, I said.

I don't think so, she said. That's not what it sounded like to
me, the way he said it.

Who said it?

Nobody. Dad.

Dad said what?

I asked him to play Chinese checkers with me and he said, I'd
rather lick the dingleberries from the cat's ass.

He was just joking, I told her. But what she said put a picture
of him in my head, him lying on the sofa, staring at the white
popcorn ceiling. Our fat gray cat curled up on his stomach.

They'd put us outside because he said he needed time alone
with Mom. Which meant sex. The thing that really sucked was
that I never knew how long the sex would be, and if we came

home before he was done he said we did it on purpose, but if we were back late we'd get in trouble because Mom worried about us.

So I had to think of something good to do. The last time, I'd brought us home too early. When I went in to check they were doing it on Siri's bed. Mom's face was pressed against the pink pillowcase, and he was grunting. Her hair was pulled back with Siri's purple ponytail holder. I got it good that time. Dad said I interrupted them on purpose.

We walked along the dirt path with our jeans rolled up past our knees. Siri's calves were more scuffed than her tennis shoes. Put your pant legs down till we get there, I told her, and she obeyed.

I was taking her to the creek. Some nights we could get there just when the sun glanced down on the water. I'd point up at the pink puffy sky. I'd say something powerful, like Behold the Bleeding Clouds. Sometimes Siri would gasp. Or hold her breath. We'd dip our feet in the cold water and fill our pockets with wet pebbles. It was a feeling hard to put into words. Like a dream curtain fell over you. It was the shimmering, we called it. Because you'd feel like you were inside the glimmering on top of the water, and kind of floaty, but not scared.

But today the creek was foamy, and it smelled of sewage. Put your shoes back on, I told Siri when she started to wiggle out of them.

What's all those bubbles? she asked me.

Soap, I said.

I couldn't decide whether to stay or go. If we stayed we could see the sunset, but the mosquitoes would come out and bite us. I decided to stay.

Behold, I said when the water turned pink, The Wine-Dark Sea.

Siri scowled. It isn't a sea, she said, and it doesn't look like wine.

Let's go home, then, I said.

We could take a bubble bath, Netti, she said.

No way. It smells like shit.

Siri knelt behind her favorite big rock and started digging for earthworms. It was past time for tadpoles. We liked collecting things out by the creek. The tadpoles hatched into little jumping toads. You couldn't keep them, they jumped too high, but you could catch one in your hands and hold it for a few minutes.

Hey look, Netti! Look what I found!

Siri held a big fat frog up to my nose. It was the palest, prettiest green, bright like a firefly's wings. Its eyes were yellow.

Wow, I said.

There's more! Look, Netti, there's more.

I'd never seen frogs like that before, but all kinds of animals came out sometimes after the floods.

What kind of toad is it? she asked.

I don't know. But it isn't a toad, I told her, it's a frog.

Siri grinned and lifted the frog up high over her head. Then she threw it against the big rock. Before I had time to say anything, she grabbed a stone as big as her fist and smashed the green frog. Its guts spilled all over.

What are you doing? You can't do that!

These frogs weren't like the toads. They were slow. She caught another and threw it into the foamy waters.

I said stop it now!

She looked up at me. Her eyes were like flat Coca-Cola. His eyes.

I don't have to, she said. I'm the boss of my own brain.

I hate you when you do bad like that, I said.

That usually got to her but it didn't this time. She went looking for another.

I'm going to mass murder all these stupid frogs, Netti, she said.

I didn't stop her. I didn't even care, right then. It seemed an okay way to fill up the long dirty time.

Galveston

THEY CAN DRIVE ALL THE WAY to Galveston if they want to, and they do. Mom ties a red scarf around her hair and rolls the windows down. The girls, Marnie and Jolene, sing songs they learned at their first Girl Scout campout last summer. They argue over the words. John Jacob Jingle Hymber Smitts or Smith. His name is my name too. Is it Smitts or Smith? It's fun to argue. They can do it for as long as they want, when their Dad isn't there, and so they do. They make up Mad-Libs in the car, they use words like Bra or Fart or Sex to make the stories funny. Mom turns on the radio. They laugh about that song the old sleaze Conway Twitty sings, "You've never been this far before."

They take the ferry and throw a loaf of bread to the gulls. Jolene watches the dolphins follow the wake of the boat and Marnie stands at the mast because she loves getting splashed. They drive all the way out to the Bolivar Peninsula.

There's a beach house for rent. It's all one room, with a little avocado-colored kitchenette and a bathroom full of seashells. They'll all share the big bed. The place smells musty but beachy, like wet sand. There's a balcony. If they'd come here in the summertime they could have slept out on the balcony. Maybe we can come in the summertime, Marnie says. Maybe we can move here. We'll put out crab traps, we can have a bonfire and make S'mores. We can plant a watermelon patch.

Mom puts it on the plastic. It's cold so everything's cheap. The ocean is gray and rolling. The best time for the beach, Mom says, we have it to ourselves. They walk to the corner store, they buy Corn Pops and weenies and canned beans. Mom buys a stack of paperback romances. They'll go out for seafood tomorrow. They'll go to the Strand and put tee shirts on the plastic.

The field around the beach house is full of sticker burrs. They run barefoot across the field, to test how much pain they can stand. They can't make it all the way to the beach, it hurts too badly. They turn back, pull out the stickers from the soles of their feet. Jolene makes monkey noises as she picks Marnie's feet. I'll bet we can harden up our feet, Marnie says. We do it enough and we'll be beach girls. It'll make hard calluses.

It's too cold to go barefoot on the beach, Mom tells them. She wears a light jacket, and the girls throw towels around their shoulders to keep warm, because they didn't pack properly. It's cold but the cold feels good, it bites them and keeps them awake. The girls dip their fingers in the water and shiver. They fill their jean pockets with shells. Mom watches, doesn't follow. Her mood is changing. She says she's pensive.

They eat Corn Pops when they get back. Mom makes them instant hot chocolate. She says the Swiss Miss looks just like her girls. The house has a radio with a cassette player, so they listen to their Dolly Parton tape, the one with "Jolene" on it, and then they listen to Crystal Gale.

It's too cold though, they can't sleep. Mom does the old trick. She opens the oven and they sit in front of it, treat it like a space heater. She makes more hot chocolate. It's fun, isn't it Mom? Marnie says. It's like a campout but better, because we're at the beach.

Mom looks bad. She's too thin, and her veins stick out too blue against her skin. She doesn't look pretty now because her face is collapsed. When she's tired, and just with the girls, sometimes her face wrinkles up into grief. The girls can't see bruises, but Marnie knows if she took her shirt off, you would see them on her back.

They sing Mom's favorite song. They try to make it good, they know she likes it when they try to sound pretty. She loves Glen Campbell. They can't remember all the words. Galveston oh Galveston, they sing. I still hear your sea winds blowing. I still see her dark eyes glowing. She was twenty-one when I left Galveston.

Do you know what that song's about? Mom asks them.

It's a love song, Marnie says.

It's about a man in Vietnam. He's afraid of dying. And he's missing the girl he loves. Isn't that sad? Mom says.

Yeah, the girls say. Time for bed, she tells them.

The mattress smells of wet dog and the sheets are sandy. They sleep in their socks and pants. Mom puts the Crystal Gale tape in again. The girls watch her through half-closed eyes. She paces. She walks in and out of the house. She walks funny, like she's drunk, or hurt, but she's not. She needs to think. At home, when he's gone, she sits in the silver light of the television with the sound turned down, and smokes. But there is no television here.

She's going to call him, Marnie whispers.

No she won't, Jolene says.

Shhh. If she walks out to the balcony one more time, she's calling him, Marnie tells her.

How do you know? Jolene asks. But Marnie always knows.

She does go out to the balcony. They can hear the ocean, even after she closes the door.

Window

JENNY LOOKS OUT HER WINDOW at the scorched grass. Rains came last night and battered the blades down. Fall is almost here, you can see it because the azalea bush is stirring in the breeze. You can see it because the kids are out on the asphalt, kicking a milk carton around. Last week would have been too hot for playing in the street. Brandy, the littlest but not the youngest, kicks the carton against Mr. Collin's gun-metal SUV. Brandy's sister Tonya runs after, skids, skins her knee. Jenny is outside with band-aids and Mercurochrome in less than five minutes.

They sit on the stoop with her, watching the blood drip. Brandy pats Tonya's knee. Her hands are sticky with blue ice pop juice.

Tonya looks at Jenny's flat belly. What happened? She asks, did your baby die?

Shut up, Tonya, Brandy says. You aren't supposed to say.

I Tell
I Don't Tell

MY PROM DATE WAS GAY. He wore a beautifully fitted tux. We went bowling instead of doing it, afterwards.

I didn't know he was gay. Not for sure. I had him pick me up at my best friend's house. My own house smelled of rotting.

I lost pregnancies.

I won't tell the details, but some are sloppy.

I used to drink too much.

That's how I met my husband.

I married for love.

But also for desperation.

This is sort of like a drinking game I once played, it was called "I Never." It always got dirty when boys played, but it was more honest when it was just girls.

I loved being a child. I was better at it than I am at being a grown up. When I met children on the playground, they all wanted to do things my way. I told them where castles and moats were and they listened.

I named them. They loved to play child catcher, slave, concubine. Slave was tag, but when someone was caught, they had to become enslaved for ten minutes. After slavery, the friends' parents would take me to Pizza Hut, Pipe Organ Pizza, or Goony Golfing. I was a good playmate for their children. I was a loyal friend. I kept secrets. At home, my mother licked envelopes. She turned all the lights off in the house to save electricity.

Thirteen was hard. I cleaned the moldy bathroom one weekend, and tried to get all the crud from out of the grout, the pee smells from the tiles around the toilet, the dead bugs out of the cupboards. I scrubbed until my nails were bleedy and the cuticles peeled back. I passed out. The reasons behind this were Tilex and anemia. My mother found me. I used to tell people this when I had been drinking. But what I said was, I almost died when I was thirteen. At least I think I did. I don't know, for sure. Because I had been drinking.

My mother said the problems were money. The problems were personality conflicts. The problems were illness, and companies that lied to us. Bosses lied to my father. The cheaters, the liars.

She knew how to cover for him. When he smashed things, and I smashed things, she would cry for us to stop. After, she cleaned up. She'd come to my room to tell me how sorry he was. I loved her more than anyone. He loves you more than anybody, she'd say. They were always saying that, how much he loved. I said she was beautiful in the dark. I wrote poems for her. I said she was cool moss under a stone. Is it good? I asked. For a girl your age it is, she told me. She was distracted.

When she asked me to leave, I took a bus. We can't afford for you to come back, she told me. I hoped he'd beat the shit out of her. They can do that, you know. She was so proud of herself, no makeup, no frivolities. She was the good one who would take care of him.

When my first love broke my heart, I drove for hours in a car I found in the junkyard. I used to sit under his dorm room window. It was softly lit with his scented candles. The dorm was in a beautiful old mansion that reminded me of *Wuthering Heights*. This college was in the woods—I had a scholarship there, and so did he. I thought we would grow old together, reading books by a fire.

My father sent him Mexican porn. What the hell is this? He said. What is this supposed to mean?

I made fun of this boyfriend at parties. I told everyone about his favorite song, the one about the sad man behind blue eyes. Then I went home and slept with Dial soap under my pillow. He used Dial soap. I sniffed it and closed my eyes. I didn't masturbate, just smelled his soap.

My best memories are of those drives I took, alone, in that beat up car. I spray-painted it Princess Pink. It came with an 8 Track and a dozen Roberta Flack tapes. I used to turn them up full blast and drive in the dark. The heat warmed my feet and I drove through rain, ice, and fog. I used to sing "Killing Me Softly." My tender heart made me feel important. I thought I was growing up and out, going places. I was on my way to something bigger.

My teacher got me on the meal plan for free. In the cafeteria, I piled my waffles high with strawberries, syrup, whip cream, all the things my mother never kept in the house. I was filling up and spilling, growing breasts, dumplings. I looked good that way, soft and pliant. Sexy. I lined my eyes in kohl and found a different boyfriend. I acquired the habit of collecting pebbles from a creek on campus, and searching for those with dark moss. I sometimes scraped the bottoms of the rocks with my teeth. The taste was awful, but it was what I craved.

World of Men

WATCH YOUR SON SPRAYING RAINBOWS in an arc, watering the flowers. Water, he says, and you hear every sound in that word. He says his Ws and Rs already, clear as the sound of that water dripping against the stones in your backyard.

Your father was a soldier. That's why, that's why, maybe he didn't know how to love right because his father was a soldier, and he hit hard. But then, your mother's father, he was also a soldier and he was nice. He taught you about car engines, and you weren't interested but pretended to be, and he bragged to the other welders, about how you loved to learn. He said you would be an engineer. He said he knew this because you never just poured the salt on your eggs without checking; you always tested the eggs first. He went to school, after the Second World War. He built his own house. He wore brown work clothes during the week and on Sundays he put a hat with a feather on it over his bald head.

Men, your mother always said, men. She said it with affection. He's a man, what can you do. Men were sweeter and simpler than women. They hit hard, loved hard. You didn't want a man who couldn't love hard. Men smelled like sweat, and needed tending. Even now, she says, you should take better care of your husband. Have you cooked him something hot? She says you are lucky to have a good man. She sighs when she says this.

You watch your son, for signs of his great grandfather. You named him for your grandfather. He likes to look inside things, see how they work. He creases his forehead in just that way, the way you almost remember. That old man, how you loved one another. The summer before he died, it was just the two of you. You made tomato soup with goldfish crackers for him almost every night. Together, you watched *M*A*S*H* and *Hill Street Blues* behind clean television trays. He did not believe in aimless television viewing. You watched three shows during the week: *Hogan's Heroes, Hill Street Blues*, and *M*A*S*H*. On weekends, Lawrence Welk. If a *Hallmark Hall of Fame* looked interesting, you circled it in the *TV Guide* and discussed its merits. In the cupboards were your grandmother's Avon lotions, apple blossom perfume, sanitary napkins, the kind with the belts. That's what you wore, you could never ask him to buy you tampons. The pads were yellowed and crumbly. At night, you heard him, restless, reckless, calling out his dead wife's name.

In the blue room, your room, there were your grandmother's things. A mink coat, heels, and dresses made of stiff material in colors from out of old movies, blue-black velvet, and maraschino red. You imagined you were she, with pearls around your neck, waiting for your soldier to come home. On Sundays, after church and breakfast at the Tanglewood, you talked to your mother. She put your father on the phone. He said he loved you. He cried. He said he was sorry. She was there, behind him, you knew, whispering the words, telling him the words to say. See, she said. See how much he loves you. She said it as if you had done something wrong to make it that way.

When your father died, his hair was long. His nails, too. It was an open casket, which was what he wanted. Your brother refused to go, but you did, and kissed his waxy forehead. You could love him this way, dead, so thin and ready to go underground.

As a girl, you ran. It was the only way, you imagined, to get away from men. Other men would take you differently. Your father knew, he said, and looked at you carefully, the way a nurse might assess her patient. You walk with too much sway, he said. You brought home blue ribbons, until your breasts grew heavier. You weren't so fast, then. And anyway, your father made you quit track. You dialed your grandfather's number, even though he was dead and gone. If he weren't, you'd be back in that house, eating tomato soup, wanting your mother but knowing you were safe. Smelling mothballs, reading in the blue room. That house was dusty, but safe.

At night you dream of your son in a desert, finding a fish. He's hungry, and he's a man now, taller than your father. His skin is burned and peeling. He needs water. You taste salt.

Your father was a diver in Vietnam. He wouldn't talk about it. But, your mother said, he saw things, things that would dissolve before they surfaced. What kinds of things? You ask. Children. You can't imagine, she always said, the world of men. The things they do.

You wake up from the dream, thirsty. It's dark outside; the baby is fast asleep. He is talking, dreaming. Fire, he says. Fire.

Harvest Moon

UNCLE TRIP SAYS he goes by the lunar calendar. He plants bulbs at night, and they take a long time to bloom. He will give me a nickel if I kiss the inside part of his palm. He says stay gold, girl, stay gold. What are you going to do with that nickel? It's not as much as the tooth fairy gives, but he's so excited about it. You can flatten it on the tracks he says. But wait, no, that's pennies.

Little girls know the secrets of the moon, he tells me. There's a man up there, did you know that?

The man in the moon is just a symbol, I tell him. From Victorian storybooks.

You know a lot, he says. What is a symbol?

I can't tell you, I explain. But I know it when I see it.

I used to think Uncle Trip was a teenager, but he isn't, he just lives at home with my grandparents. He has a pet tarantula, and he let me hold it once. He put it on the back of my neck. It felt like long, tiny fingers tickling. I was nervous but also excited, like the way I felt when we flew to Florida and the plane took off, and I felt a bump in the sky.

Uncle Trip has hazel eyes, exactly my color of hazel. He has hair like a doll's, like plastic hair that's been brushed so often it frizzes out. He built me a dollhouse out of shoeboxes. I really am not interested in dolls, but the house was interesting. He used Pez candies for tiles, and he put in little tiny stickers that were pictures of our family on the walls. It was very intricate. He made it for me but I'm not supposed to bring it home. It stays for visits. He asked wouldn't I like to live in that shoebox house, if nobody could find us, and we would not ever have to worry about food or feelings because we could be dolls. Dolls have a sort of immortality. We could be dolls with souls, he said.

He says, stay gold. Little girls know the secrets, little girls like things for their beauty. Like you, you like a music box because it is lovely, because you dream of being a ballerina.

Not anymore, I explain. I'm going to be a journalist or a country western singer, or a nun.

Don't give in to vanity, he says. Girls turn thirteen now and then they smell like a ladies bathroom. All pink and bloody, and artificial. They stink and then they cover up the stink.

Sun

My father sends me pieces of the letter in postcards. The first card says, *I am in* and then the second says *Poland* even though he sent it from Toronto. Which, maybe he doesn't know this, but is just as foreign to me as Poland.

He sends me an envelope filled with petals. I ask my mother what kind of flower they are from. She looks at me with shiny eyes. That's the way she cries, squinting so that her eyes don't run. She whispers on the phone to my aunt, she thinks I can't hear or maybe she knows I can, she just thinks it would be improper to say it above a hiss. Onanistic, she says. I look up the word—it means coitus interuptus or masturbation. She never went to college, but she reads a lot and maybe she thinks she's using the word properly but I'm not sure. Maybe she means, it's all masturbation, him being around us.

He stayed with us for one week, a week in June. He gave me a nickname right away, called me Junebug. He wasn't like any of my mother's friends; his hair was cut to look shaggy, falling over his left eye in a sultry way. He smelled of kitchen spices. He said we had the same eyes. Not the color, he said, the shape. Once, when I was pretending to sleep, he came into my room and kissed my eyelids. It was weird, but nice, like a feather duster tickling.

So Toronto, I imagine, has very green grass and good coffee and it must feel clean and crisp to walk out there and not hot and sleepy, like it does down here. He told me that the sun is more direct in Texas. We were in a park, my Mom was buying us mango snow cones and we were lying on our backs, looking up at the sun. He is the kind of man who can do that without looking foolish. I looked up at the sky until my eyes hurt and then knit my fingers in front of my face. He told me he'd wanted to name me Iris, which was his mother's favorite flower.

The third postcard is from Austin, Texas. Not far away, not more than two hundred miles away. It's a photo of a bunch of people in burlap halters and dirty shorts dancing around bongos. *Eeyore's Birthday Party*, it says. *I haven't been to Poland in a long time*, it says. I don't remember your birth date but I remember the day you were born. You made little fists and blew me bubbles.

The next postcard is just a corny painting of a bunch of flowers. I don't know what kind they are, they look like wild flowers. It says, *You almost make me want to go legit.*

I don't show that to her. I hope she doesn't see the cards before I do. I check the mail every week day as soon as I get home from school but I think she's onto me.

The letter is never finished. I get another one, this time a card of rainbows and unicorns, and it says *If I'm right you are not a rainbow and unicorns kind of girl. That's a good thing. I imagine most girls like that grow up to be dental hygienists and Dallas Cowgirls. But I'm in a card shop and I asked Dorothy, the saleswoman, to direct me to cards for a girl of fourteen and this is where she*

That's the last card. The words are so tiny and crowded, I can barely make them out. I'm a sucker, I tell my mom. That week he stayed with us, she made him iced coffee with condensed milk the way they used to drink it together that summer he lived with her. One night, they went out to hear music and that's the night he kissed my eyelids. That thing he said about Dallas Cowgirls was pretty nasty because when she was in high school, my mother was a drill team captain. She wore shining pantyhose and white boots up to her knees, and marched in the Cotton Bowl.

"He thinks he's so quirky, but really, he is very obvious," I say to her. She brushes my hair back, and then lets her palm rest in the nape of my neck, like a hug. I'm writing a report about the sun and the moon, and I keep on writing and she keeps her hand there for a long time.

There's going to be a solar eclipse this Saturday. You're supposed to look at it through cardboard, with your back turned. I tell her that's what I'm going to do. But I intend to look at it directly.

The Sky Is a Well

IT IS THE NIGHT BEFORE CHRISTMAS. My brother has his stocking on his head. He thinks that is what a stocking cap is. I show him the picture from our Little Golden Book. A stocking cap, I tell him, is what old men wore in the days of yore. They also wore nightgowns. Our own father sleeps in the nude. Friends' fathers wear pajamas, or boxers. Only ladies wear nightgowns, my brother says. But he knows that if I tell him something, it is probably true.

There are pudding pops in the freezer. We each take one, then tiptoe outside in our bare feet. Or, as my brother calls it, berry feet. It's too warm for Christmas. Too cold, really, for bare feet. The pudding pop sends icicles through my teeth and pierces the top of my skull. Brain freeze, my brother says.

Every Christmas I pray for snow, but I'm beginning to think that is unrealistic. God probably doesn't bring snow to the desert unless you are, say, a prophet spreading His Word. Or at least a saint. Or a beautiful, innocent child. I am not innocent, and I'm cute, at best.

Under a gnarled mesquite tree is our sin. I've buried our sins for us in little scraps of paper. There is also a small puppy there, one we found on the side of the road after a hard cold night. He'd probably frozen to death, I explained. My brother is too little to write his sins for himself so I wrote them for him. But he is too good, he's never done anything really bad. Here is what I write for him: I used a popgun in the house. I passed some gas at the table and said it was my sister. Sometimes I get so mad and I want to hit someone. I had a frog and I didn't feed him, and then he ran away.

My sins are folded into doves and stars. I won't tell him what they are. I hope, buried beneath the earth, they tangle up with the roots of the tree. I want them to stay down there, get strangled by the roots and eaten by worms. One night, I dreamt the doves came alive, tried to chirp, then suffocated. Evil, dark, dank thoughts.

I'm cold, my brother tells me.

Wave to the moon, I tell him. And make a wish.

We look up at the moon. She's shivering in between branches of our little tree.

Angel Wings

MY FATHER WASN'T HOME. He had been gone for almost three days this time. When he came home sometimes he tickled me until I almost peed in my pants. But when he was gone, I felt calm. I stuck my tongue into the groove where my front tooth had been. It tasted good, kind of sweet and rusty.

My father had punched the tooth out. Nobody asked about it. They just assumed I'd lost it. Not telling wasn't lying. Your father has never told a single lie, my mother told me. As she said this she swallowed, hard, and looked straight ahead.

She said that loving a great man wasn't easy, but she knew, in her heart, it was the path God had chosen for her. Sometimes I sat on the stoop with her while she smoked. I liked the way she tapped the cigarette case against the steps. Her lips were stained Wine on Ice, a red deeper than blood. Lipstick was all she ever wore on her face. That was something her mother taught her, she said. Less can be more. Don't let them think you try too hard. I listened carefully. When she smoked she seemed different, not the lady she was when my father was home. "Everyone has their vices," she told me, "you don't need to tell Daddy about this."

It felt important, sharing her secret. She looked out at the road as if she was waiting for someone.

We had other secrets, too. Sometimes, on the Sundays when my father was gone and she was too tired, we watched Oral Roberts instead of going to church.

We'd decided together that I was going to be an angel for Halloween. The Littlest Angel. The Littlest Angel gave Jesus a collection of his most favorite things. A robin's egg, a tiger's eye marble, a catcher's mitt.

My mother told me the story of the Littlest Angel almost every night. "And what would you present to God, as your gift?" she asked me. This was a serious question and I thought about it for a long time.

I imagined the list of things I would present to God. There were the angel wings my grandmother had made for me three months before she fell down the stairs at Luby's, broke her hip, went to the hospital and never made it out again. The wings were white mesh with silver slivers all over and real white feathers around the edges.

The other things on my list weren't mine. The porcelain cat the color of orange marmalade that stayed over the fake fireplace mantle in the living room. Her name was Marmy and she licked her tiny paw as demurely as my grandmother used to pull off her driving gloves with her fingertips. A lavender brush that sat on my mother's dresser. It smelled of Tuberose perfume. I still hadn't decided what else should be on the list.

It was getting late. My mother sat watching *The Lawrence Welk Show* in the living room. I was hungry, but I knew she was sad so I turned on my Lite Brite and fed my pet doodlebugs and waited. After a long time I went into the living room. She was sitting on the floor in the dark. The television flickered bluish light across her face.

"It's dark in here," I told her.

"My head hurts, Laura. Can you go back in your room and play while I have a rest?"

"Okay. But I'm scared of the dark."

"Turn on your light, then," she told me.

I left her alone. My doodlebugs lived in a flowerpot in my windowsill. I pulled out the little cars from the Game of Life and put Cheesika, the littlest doodlebug, into the pink car. Rain pelted the window and the raindrops ran down in streams across the windowpane. They made a good lake for Cheesika to drive over.

Thunder clapped and sheet lightening struck. The Lite Brite went out. I was still. I lowered Cheesika carefully into the flowerpot. I couldn't see her crawl into the dirt. I called out to my mother, but she didn't answer.

I walked slowly back into the living room.

"Mommy?"

She was still there, sitting Indian style on the floor. All the lights were out.

"The power went out," she said.

"I bumped my leg," I lied.

"You should have waited for your eyes to adjust."

"Can you write my list for me?" I asked her.

She sighed. "It's bedtime, anyway."

She stared at the dark television screen as if there were light in it. I didn't say anything. I walked over to the window and stood in front of it for a long time. I stared at the punched-out black night. Then I pressed my palms against the windowpane and felt its cool hard surface. I stuck my tongue into the groove in my gum. The glass felt just the way my groove tasted. Cold and hard, a deep, sweet ache.

Arson

WHEN I CAN'T SLEEP, and I'm alone, I think about the people I hate until I don't hate them anymore. Then I feel guilty for hating them. Then I think, wait a minute, that fuck, he did that, she did that — it goes back and forth, me hating them and then remembering how I loved them. After I spent all that time hating, I usually dream about people who don't matter much. Like the woman I worked with in a bookstore ten years ago, who was married to someone who didn't want children. She wore Barney tee shirts and inventoried the children's section. I don't remember her name, but, in my dream, we are sisters. We are both blonde. We are both pregnant. I look like her, or at least the way I remember her. My eyes are soft focus, blue. My skin is milky. I'm plump all over, but pretty, and sleepy-eyed. My father is not my father, in this dream. He is our father. But wait a minute, he's driving a milk truck and telling me I have to nurse a bunch of puppies. I say no, bestiality is disgusting. He asks me why I have dyed my hair. My long blonde hair starts falling out, and now my father is no longer a nice looking milkman, he is my real father. Damn, he ruined my dream. I'm not having sex with you, I tell him. Pull over and let me out of this car.

But where will you go? Where would you be without me?

See what he does, getting into my dream like that. When I wake up, my hair will be short, not long. Not long the way it was back then.

When I was a child, there was a fire two doors down. A family died. A mother, a father, and a baby boy. And another woman, of shady character. The father was having an affair with the woman.

We all have our limits, my mother said. I would never stay with your father if he cheated on me. He knows that.

I couldn't imagine anyone wanting to have an affair with my father. He didn't clip his toenails. He walked around the house, naked, talking about nudism. He said I should be happy to have parents who loved one another. He cupped my mother's breasts at the table. You're just jealous, he told me.

I played softball. I was good at it. I didn't talk to the other girls. I didn't know what to say to them. I never even had to practice, I hit the ball just about every time. The family that burned, it wasn't arson. It was an accident. The mother fell asleep with her cigarette lit.

That's why your father and I don't smoke. And because it's unhealthy.

In another dream, my mother and I are twin sisters. We both have long blonde hair. I'm sure you'll be a good mother, my mother tells me. We're both pregnant.

The fire was real. It wasn't a dream. The boy's name was Arthur, and I babysat for him. He wasn't a baby, he was four years old. But I thought of him that way. We watched *He-Man* together, and I told him the story of *Black Beauty*.

I was thirteen. I thought I would die, feeling the way I felt. I wrote a story about a girl whose father fucked her, and my father said, it's her fantasy. I wanted to die. My mother said, we're on your side. You know that.

But when I watched that kid, I felt smart. And cool. I could be the cool babysitter, the one who made chocolate cookies and told the best stories. I brought him Milk Duds.

It was, I believed, the worst thing that ever happened to me, when that little boy died. I wasn't his mother, or his sister. I was just his babysitter.

He never should have brought that other woman into his house, my mother said.

Oh, why don't you stop it, I said. You don't know what happened.

I think about my ex-boyfriend, how he dumped me before his graduation, then brought my roommate with him to introduce to his mother. I think about the way he masturbated into his socks, and how poor his grades were.

He was a terrible student. He never paid rent on time. He never drank beer, he drank "ale" and "port wine." He thought he saw William Blake in the clouds. Because he was always tripping. There, that's better. Stick with that one.

Her Lips

PRAYING HANDS ON A CEDAR BOX. I kept it empty, because nothing seemed important enough for it. I liked to close my eyes and sniff the wood. With my eyes closed, the box was a forest and I was inside.

My husband tells me I'm a target, the way I lean forward, courting everyone. We are just married. He thought that was all for him. I tell him that the world is my target. Everyone will love me. I read about Marilyn, how she wanted to be the most beautiful woman in the room, and how she was. Even though she wasn't. I don't want to be the most anything, I say. Good, because you aren't. He's angry.

My impression of Marilyn, my husband tells me, was that she acted with her lips.

He wants me to tell him something I don't tell everyone, some story that hasn't taken shape yet. I tell him about the cedar box. Is that true? He asks me.

Yes, only I'm not sure about the part where I close my eyes and there's a forest.

But that's the best part, he says.

Well, it's true now. We are lying down on a mattress with the covers pulled up to our necks. My dog, now our dog, wants to climb in bed with us but there's no room. It's a twin. Lie down, Daffodil, I tell her.

I take my clothes off under the covers. It's cold. With my eyes closed, I can feel him better. He smells of smoke and musk. His heart under my ear. I'm not drinking again, I tell him. I won't tell any secrets to anyone but you, ever again.

He's falling into sleep. The dog is snoring. I want to get up, get out. Go out in the cold and walk to a bar, where there's a only a few and I don't know them.

About the Author

Claudia Smith lives in San Antonio, Texas with her husband and son. Twice nominated for the Pushcart Prize, her fiction has appeared in *Redivider, The Mississippi Review* online, *Juked, Night Train, Elimae,* and *Sou'wester,* among others. Her stories have been anthologized in Norton's *New Sudden Fiction: Short-Short Stories from America and Beyond* and So New Media's *Consumed: Women on Excess.* More about Claudia and her work can be found at www.claudiaweb.net.

A Note About the Type

The interior of this book is set in Sabon. Often described as a Garamond revival and considered one of the most legible text faces, it was designed by the renowned German type designer Jan Tschichold in 1964. The design is based on a set of cuts by Claude Garamond (c. 1480–1561) that were printed on a specimen sheet by Frankfurt printer Konrad Berner. Berner married the widow of type designer and fellow printer Jacques Sabon, who was one of Garamond's assistants and the namesake for this elegant typeface.

—*Melissa Gruntkosky*